I0671490

Copyright © 2024 by Abigail Kelly

Cover and interior illustrations © 2024 by Abigail Kelly

All rights reserved.

No part of this book may be reproduced in any form or by any electronic or mechanical means, including information storage and retrieval systems, without written permission from the author, except for the use of brief quotations in a book review. No part of this book or its illustrations were created with AI and no part of it may be used to train, inspire, or otherwise assist in the creation of AI content.

SANGUINE

THE NEW PROTECTORATE STORIES: VOLUME SIX

ABIGAIL KELLY

AUTHOR'S NOTE

Sanguine is a standalone novella within the wider *New Protectorate Series* and can be read as such. However, it does contain some spoilers for other books in the series, particularly *Empire*. A full reading list and character directory can be found at abigailkkelly.com. Content warnings can also be found there, as well as in the backmatter of this book, alongside a glossary.

~Abigail

For the caged.

PROLOGUE

An excerpt from an article titled "Blood Bride Ring Busted: Grim's Priest Arrested On Charges of Imprisonment And Sale Of Sentient Beings" by Bob Sasini published in *The San Francisco Light*:

Yesterday, at approximately 7PM EST, authorities of the Department of Citizen Protection raided a small crypt in Moorseville, North Carolina and arrested four people on suspicion of running a blood bride trafficking operation. One of those arrested was High Priest Mitchell Hoyer, a vampire who ran the crypt and its attached funeral home for close to ninety years. Four others were arrested as well, including acolytes and employees. A handful of suspects, including a woman known as the matron, are currently being pursued and are expected to be apprehended in the next 24 hours.

According to a credible source close to the investigation, the Neutral Zone's CPD has been surveilling the Mooresville crypt for years, mostly for workers' rights violations and money laundering. It was a tip-off from an insider that propelled the investigation into its active phase with the CPD's vampire task force.

The insider claims agents discovered several rooms within the crypt that suggest several people were living there off the record.

"I can't share any details," the source told us in a quick phone call last night, "but investigators have been able to track down a few brides already by tracing some of the money. There might have been ten vampires in the crypt at one time, but there were probably a lot more in and out over the years. The rumor is that most of them have been there since they were kids."

When asked why no one reported any suspicious behavior, the source claimed that the captives were dressed and trained as acolytes of the goddess of death herself. They worked in the funeral home and tended the temple within the crypt. "No one would have known by looking at them," they said. "They looked just like every other acolyte."

But they weren't just devotees to Grim. They were blood brides, and they lived in plain sight, ready to be sold to the highest bidder whenever the time came.

For San Franciscans and other citizens of the Elvish Protectorate who might be unfamiliar with it, *blood bride* is a gender-inclusive term that refers to a venom neutral vampire mated — or intended to be mated — to another vampire. Normally, two vampires could never feed on one another or reproduce, since their venom and blood is fatal when ingested by one of their own kind.

Due to a rare genetic quirk, a bride can act as an anchor — a vampire's mate — in exactly the same way another being can. They have no trouble producing vampiric offspring, which has made them a target of vampiric bloodline purists for centuries.

The blood bride trade has been in business for a very long time, and Grim's acolytes, known for their commitment to the dead and worship of the goddess through celibacy, have historically denounced it and supported it in equal measures. Vampiric culture has also changed its level of tolerance toward the practice many times.

Today, it's mostly seen as the domain of zealots, criminals looking to legitimize their bloodline, and the most vulnerable — those who are forced to give their children up to be brides, either for money or simply through the inability to protect them, and those who volunteer themselves for similar reasons.

The trade has been outlawed in most countries for at least two-hundred years, but there are enormous amounts of money to be made from wealthy vampires seeking to add prestige to their bloodlines. The EVP has strict laws against the practice. However, due to the territory's incredibly low vampire population, it's a rare case that makes it to court. Most blood bride trafficking happens in the Neutral Zone, where the largest number of vampires in the world resides.

The penalties for trafficking blood brides are steep, which is probably why, when High Priest Hoyer got wind of the upcoming raid, he allegedly acted swiftly to sell off the brides in the crypt's possession. "There were at least six just a couple weeks ago," the source said, his frustration evident. "But now they're all gone. I really hope the investigators can track them down. Or else the gods only know where they'll end up."

Chapter One

It was a bad idea to take the job. Atticus felt it in his bones the moment he stepped out of the car and into the deserted parking lot.

Mr. Junger said it was a nothing job for someone like him. He agreed. He'd been trained and served under the command of his adopted father, Harlan Bounds, since he was a scrawny preteen picking pockets for synth money. He'd been forged into a weapon, a hunter, and an assassin whenever necessary. This kind of job was so far below his pay grade, it was basically charity.

"It's just a transport gig," Junger had assured him. *"Nothing illegal, but something precious. I need a good, honorable man to bring it to me. Someone who won't stab me in the back the first chance he gets."*

Atticus would never go so far as to say he was good or honorable, but he was raised to be a man of his word, and he didn't fuck around on clients. That was the quickest way to get a bolt through the brain, and he liked his brain how it was. Mostly.

He wouldn't have said he trusted Junger, who was little more than a friend of an acquaintance, but he also wouldn't have taken the job if he thought there was anything unusual about it. Hubert Junger was a businessman who owned a small chain of synth manufacturing plants in the Sacramento area. He was a vampire, just as Atticus was, and kept his nose clean with the law. Sure, he was a bit of a blow-hard, and he'd definitely fallen into that vampiric trap of obsession over his legacy, but he had money and a job that would get Atticus away from home for a while. That was exactly what he was after.

There was nothing wrong with home. He liked it a lot, actually, but he'd been restless lately. Short-tempered and anti-social. So much so that Harlan took him aside and asked him if he needed a break from working security detail on the estate.

The memory burned. Atticus imagined shame felt a bit like acid reflux, though he'd never actually experienced it.

He didn't need a break from work. He loved keeping his people safe. But that didn't mean he was satisfied with his life. Not completely. He didn't want to keep coming home to an empty house every morning. He was tired of staring at his ceiling, wondering if he should be more grateful for the gifts he'd been given and why he felt like such an outsider, a voyeur looking in on other people's happiness.

His sister was safe, even if she'd run to live as far from them as she could get. Harlan was blissed out every damn minute of the night thanks to his anchor, Zia. Atticus himself had a full belly and a roof over his head. What was there to long for?

Something of his own. His own reason to come home every morning. His own life to be proud of. His own family, maybe, or something else that could make him feel like he wasn't just coasting through life, waiting for the next shoe to drop.

So no, he didn't need a *vacation*, but he didn't want Harlan to feel like he needed to apologize for his growing family and shifting priorities, so he agreed to some time off. A quick, safe job would get his head on straight.

There was no outward sign that this job wouldn't fit the bill. There was no sign of anything at all. The gas station was brightly lit but deserted. The blacktop was cracked and stained with puddles of oil. Old paper signs nearly covered the windows of the building.

There were no other cars.

A cold crawling feeling started up the back of his neck as he surveyed the darkness around the station. The glow barely made a dent in the yawning blackness of the desert stretching all around them. He stood at the very edge of an island of light. The closest town was a forty-five minute drive back the way he came, and the nearest city was hours and hours away.

Atticus adjusted the strap of his backpack over his shoulders, then checked the gun holstered at his side. And the one at his right ankle. And then the knife strapped to his thigh.

It made no sense for anything to be up, not when Junger had passed his background check with only a few unsavory notes in the margins, but vampires were wily, spiteful, and often didn't even know what they were going to do until they did it. Atticus learned very early on to trust no one but family.

The low rumble of an engine broke the silence. He half-turned toward the road that connected to the other side of the lot. Twin dots of light that began as pinpricks in the far distance gradually got bigger.

The muscles of Atticus's neck tensed, but his arms remained loose. Ready.

A frigid wind whipped off the hard-packed desert soil and sent the hem of his long coat fluttering. Bits of grit sprayed his cheeks as he watched the vehicle gradually resolve against the velvet blackness of the night.

Junger said he'd be driving a van, and he was apparently true to his word. It was one of those fancy miniature RVs that pulled into the lot, its headlights turned down low. Hitched to the back was some sort of sleek trailer about half the size of the van.

The RV pulled up next to Atticus's borrowed car. The engine cut. For just a moment, there were no other sounds but the howl of the wind and his own breathing.

Then the door opened.

A pale, upper-middle aged woman hopped out of the driver's seat and didn't bother shutting the door. Her face was a little gaunt, her eyes restless as they assessed Atticus, then his car, then the lot, before doing the circuit all over again. One fang worried her chapped bottom lip.

"Well?"

Atticus glanced at the trailer again. There was nothing distinct about it. Nothing outwardly strange, except for the units attached to the front and top. Maybe it was refrigerated?

It wasn't his place to speculate, though, so he grunted the codeword Junger had given him. "Stitches."

The woman nodded. Smoothing her palms down the front of her jeans, she started walking toward the car. "Good. Okay. Safe trip."

"Wait." Atticus caught her arm before the woman could scuttle into the car and haul ass out of there. "How do I know the cargo is in there? You got a key or something to that trailer?"

The woman gave him a narrow-eyed look and lifted her lip to show her fangs. "It's in there. And your biometrics were keyed into the lock in case of an emergency. You're not supposed to look, though. Your boss was very clear about that."

Your boss. Atticus had to work hard to keep the tendons in his neck from popping out.

Junger wasn't his boss. He was nobody. Atticus had one boss, one man in the whole world he respected above all others, and that was Harlan fucking Bounds. To imply he answered to anyone else was galling.

Taking this job was a mistake. That cold crawling feeling sharpened, spread down from his neck to his whole spine.

This wasn't supposed to be an illegal job, just under the table transport. He'd left crime behind when he, his sister Adriana, and Harlan escaped the vampire syndicate several years prior. Adriana had never, ever been part of it, but he and Harlan were once the two most sought after assassins on the continent, as long as you didn't count Shade, a jack-of-all-trades madman.

They'd given that life up — happily, more or less — for safety and security in the Elvish Protectorate, leaving United Washington and its vampiric underbelly behind.

But the way the other vampire was looking at him now, the trailer, the gut feeling swirling inside Atticus... It was all too familiar. Too close to all those jobs he'd done to survive before Harlan saved his ass.

But what could he do? He'd already given his word, and something about getting back in that car, leaving the trailer behind, made his stomach clench.

Atticus let the woman go with a grunt. "If something's wrong, then it's your ass who's gonna pay the price. Got it?"

"Good luck," the woman dared to sneer, but she wasn't brave enough to stick around. Bony shoulders hunched around her ears, she hustled off toward the car. Atticus watched her practically throw herself into the driver's seat. The tires screeched as she pulled onto the road. The scent of burnt rubber lingered for a moment before the wind blew it away.

Running his claws through his windswept hair, Atticus let out a sigh. "Well, fuck."

Chapter Two

The rules were simple:

1. Get the cargo.
2. Drive, avoiding all major checkpoints that couldn't be bribed.
3. No stops at hotels or in cities.
4. Don't look in the trailer.

Atticus made it about two hours before he decided to break rule number four.

Knowing that Junger was a regular, if sleazy, businessman had lulled him into a false sense of security. Atticus had guessed he'd be transporting some weird sex thing, or art Junger wasn't supposed to have, or illegal parts to a foreign vehicle, or some special synth ingredient he wanted smuggled in so he didn't have to pay high EVP taxes on it.

Until the hand-off, his money was on the sex thing.

He kept glancing in the rearview mirror of the RV. The sight of the trailer never revealed anything new, but every time he looked at it, the hair on the back of his neck stood up.

He knew better than to poke his nose in other people's shit. That was the quickest way to get it on your face.

But the longer he drove down the desolate stretch of road that wound like a gray river through the desert, the harder he found it to ignore his gut. He lived by his word. He suspected he'd probably die by it, too. But did his word mean shit if he was suckered into something he didn't consent to?

And didn't his word to stay safe, to not jeopardize his family, mean more than an agreement with a shitty old man like Junger?

Atticus checked the time on the glowing dashboard console. The sun would rise soon, and he'd have to pull off. He'd need to pull down the blackout shades on the windows. The sun wouldn't kill him — not for a while, at least, since only the infirm and babies were at risk of immediate death — but burns hurt like a motherfucker, especially when it was delivered by the vicious animal that was the desert sun. Even in the fall, it was a bitch.

He'd have to pull off. He'd have to rest. He'd be stuck in the tin can of the luxury, compact RV all day. It wasn't a prospect that bothered him before, but now that he had no idea what he'd gotten himself into, he found the idea of being stuck in the desert with the mysterious cargo not quite as appealing as before.

Atticus checked the time again. He had about an hour left.

If I pull off and just take a quick peek, I'll be fine. It was stupid to have this much anxiety over the contents of a trailer. Even if something extremely illegal was inside, he'd almost certainly seen worse. The annoying part would be handling the fallout if it turned out it was worth breaking his word over.

He shook his head. He'd been out of the game too long if something like a little illegal cargo could rattle him this bad.

A wry smile tugged at his lips. If part of this little break from estate security life had been about discovering if he really missed the criminal world or not, he supposed that question had been answered.

He glanced in the mirror again, then looked at the time.

Hissing through his fangs, he scowled at the road, scouting for a good place to pull off and keep out of sight of any traffic. Not that he expected there to be much, but the last thing he needed was a long-haul trucker asking questions.

It was smart for a number of reasons to give him an RV and a trailer. Not only was it completely self-contained and left no money trail, if anyone pulled him over, he could say he was just camping in the desert. It wasn't technically a lie, especially when he found a spot to turn off and tuck the RV behind a scraggly hill.

The vehicle bumped and rattled over rocks and the divots left-over from monsoon floods. He grunted every time it lurched, his knuckles gone white around the steering wheel, and hoped that whatever was in the trailer wasn't fragile.

It was a relief when he finally cut the engine. Releasing his seatbelt, Atticus sat for a second to really, really be sure he wanted to do this before he sighed again, checked that his bolt gun had a full battery, and opened the door.

His boots crunched on the loose, sunbaked topsoil as he made his way around the back of the RV. He scanned the trailer again. Nothing was weird about it.

It looked a bit like the ones used to haul expensive equipment, or a very rich man's dirt bikes. That didn't exactly explain the units on the front and roof, but who knew what weird shit rich people got into when they started buying toys.

He'd made a lot of money over the years, but he'd never fallen into the trap of buying dumb stuff. Murder paid well, and Harlan was a ruthless investor and shrewd businessman. He'd taught Atticus and Adriana how to handle their money responsibly.

Atticus *could* buy whatever he wanted. Trouble was that he didn't want much — a nice house, a fast car, and maybe a woman who didn't mind being bitten every night. He was a simple man with simple needs.

Or maybe not. If it really was so simple, why couldn't he be satisfied with what he had? It sure as shit would have kept him out of whatever mess he'd stepped into.

Shoulders back and arms loose, Atticus carefully slipped his gun free of its holster and clicked off the safety. Somewhere a little too close for comfort, a coyote's screaming howl erupted, putting his fangs more on edge.

He hesitated at the back of the trailer. The cargo was only to be accessed in case of an emergency. Junger had been very firm on that point. If there was a crash, an attack, or if for some reason the trip lasted more than seven days, he was allowed to unlock it. If not, then...

This could be a colossal mistake.

His jaw firmed. It *already* felt like a mistake taking the job. How much worse could he do, really?

A lot. He could do a *lot* worse, actually.

Atticus hesitated. He didn't want any blowback from his stupid decisions to hit Harlan and Zia, his adopted father's anchor. They were starting a family. He didn't want it to hit his sister, either, who already had to live her life smothered in secrecy because of a random genetic quirk.

So he didn't open the lock right away. Instead, for reasons he couldn't even explain to himself, he knocked.

Two quick raps on the metal door, then he stepped back, gun raised. At first, nothing happened. He felt like an idiot. Of course nothing happened. There was no one there. It was an equipment trailer, not a—

Bang! Bang!

His shoulders tensed. Blood drained from his face as the knocking continued, the rhythm growing faster. It sounded like someone was trying to beat their way out.

There's a person in there.

His first instinct was to lunge for the door and release whoever was locked inside, but he'd long ago learned that acting on impulse often led to mistakes. A good killer used their head and their gut in concert, not one or the other all on its own.

Keeping his gun high, he barked, "Who's in there? Give me a name."

There was no response, just more pounding. The beat was erratic, like the person inside was desperate but could only maintain it for so long before their arm got tired or their hand hurt too much. He knew from experience that pounding on a locked door for long periods of time could hurt like a bitch.

"Stop knocking and answer me," he demanded. But there was no significant breakup in the beat, so he guessed that whoever it was inside, they probably couldn't hear him.

Fucking fuck. Atticus hissed and lowered his gun just enough to start fiddling with the lock. He wasn't super great with technology, so it took him a second to figure out all the steps it required to unlock it.

There was a series of flashing lights, some beeps, and then the smooth grinding sound of heavy bolts sliding across metal. The knocking stopped.

Raising his gun again, Atticus grasped the large metal latch on the door and yanked. He stepped back quickly, allowing it to swing open, and leveled the barrel of his gun at opening.

A waft of scent rushed out. Clean skin. Something a little waxy. A heady, sweet, earthy sort of scent he couldn't place but immediately made his mouth water.

And inside the darkness of the trailer, untouched by moonlight, were a pair of reflective eyes.

He almost forgot about where he was, that he had a gun in his hands, when a face, pale as a porcelain doll's, came into view around those eyes. A sloping forehead ran into a pert nose and dark eyebrows. Proud cheekbones made an already round face a little bit rounder. A soft, small mouth crowned a narrow chin.

Her skin was unnaturally pale and looked even more so in comparison to the red circles painted onto her chin and forehead. Her lips were painted, too.

She was huddled on the floor of the trailer, most of her body obscured by a long white dress and — he did a doubletake — a mind-boggling fall of raven black hair. Small hands, also painted white with red circles on the backs and tipped with red polish, curled defensively around her knees.

Her shoulders moved with her rapid breaths, and when he

looked back at her face, he found her expression rigid and her eyes so wide, he could make out white all around.

Her gaze flicked to the gun. Before he could figure out how to unglue his tongue from the roof of his mouth, she asked, "Are you my groom?"

Atticus dropped his arms immediately, pointing the gun at the ground rather than the— His stomach rebelled so hard, he worried he might actually get sick right there in the dirt.

A blood bride. I was hired to bring Junger a blood bride.

Looking back, the job being about a weird sex thing would have been vastly preferable to *this*. He didn't fuck around with blood brides, not when the very concept was a threat to his sister. In another world, she would have ended up exactly like this woman: dolled up to look like an acolyte of the goddess Grim, tossed into the back of a fucking trailer, and dragged to the other side of the continent to become some sleazy businessman's broodmare.

He'd always found the idea of people wanting a pure vampiric bloodline deeply gross. Even if Adriana hadn't been born with the gene that allowed her to produce offspring with another vampire, he still would have found it disgusting.

But there he was, complicit in the very practice he'd worked all his life to save his sister from.

His throat had closed up. He couldn't speak or even make a noise. All he could do was stare at the woman in horror, his gun aimed at the dirt and his shoulders so stiff, it felt like the muscles had turned to stone.

But the longer he remained silent, the more unsettled she became. He could see it happening, but he was helpless to stop it. Her eyes bounced between his and the gun, then to the wide expanse of the desert behind him.

Shock hadn't just robbed him of his ability to speak. It also made him painfully slow.

That was the only explanation for why he lunged for her a second too late.

The bride sprang out of the back of the trailer. Swathed in all that fabric, barefoot, and dragging nearly her full height in hair, one wouldn't think that she'd be so quick, but damn if she didn't smoke his ass.

Instinct revved to life. The drive to hunt prey was, when provoked, one of the most intense in vampires. The only urge that came second to it was the craving to find an anchor, a mate to sip from and breed.

Atticus holstered his gun. His mind shut down as he followed the streak of white across the rocky desert ground. His vision tunneled. Nothing else mattered but the shape of her back, the whip of her hair over her shoulder, and that lush scent he drew into his lungs with great, heaving breaths.

There were no real thoughts running through his mind. Just impressions. Needs.

He saw only her. He felt only his need to catch her. He needed to make sure she didn't damage her bare feet on the ground. He needed more of that scent. He needed to get them both out of the open before the sun hit the horizon.

That last need was the one that brought back a sliver of rationality. His heart seized as he risked a glance at the sky. It was already beginning to turn a deep, navy blue.

Just as fast, his focus was back on his runaway. Panic burned through him as he watched her fly over jagged rocks, toward nothing but more desert, less shelter. If he lost her, if he couldn't get them back to the RV in time, there was a good chance she could be hurt. If she escaped him completely, she could die.

"Stop!" he bellowed, knowing good and well that it was a stupid thing to say to someone who had no reason to listen.

She didn't stop, but she stumbled. Hard.

Atticus cursed as he watched her go down. He was a bit too far away to see why, but he thought she might have stepped on something. Gods only knew what was out in the desert. It wasn't just jagged rocks, but bits of old barbed wire fence, the detritus left over from the war, broken glass, and rusty nails.

Alarm pushed him to go faster, the fastest he'd ever run before, despite the fact that she was struggling to stand.

He was on her in seconds.

She shrieked when he skidded down beside her, one leg outstretched and the other bent to hold his weight. His boots sent a cloud of dust and grit into the air. He slapped his hands onto the ground to stop his momentum and ended up nearly on top of her as she scrambled backward, trying to crawl away.

"*Stop,*" he grunted, trying and mostly failing to not snarl at her. She didn't stop, of course, so he was forced to grab one of her ankles and drag her back to him. "Just fucking *listen* for a second! I'm not going to hurt you!"

She fought like a hellion there in the dirt, with her little red claws and her bleeding feet. He would have been impressed with how many blows she managed to land if he weren't counting down the minutes until sunrise — and also hard as steel behind his fly. The urge to subdue her with his weight and drive his aching fangs into her throat was a great, throbbing need in his mind, blocking out nearly everything else.

Atticus cursed and fought to grab both her wrists with one hand. Once he had her, it wasn't too hard to pin her down. She was as fine-boned as a bird. It took barely any effort at all to hold her still as he straddled her middle, using his much greater weight to stop her thrashing.

"Hey. *Hey!*" He didn't like having to shake her, but when she kept trying to angle her head to bite his arm, he didn't exactly have a choice. Even knowing she was most likely venom neutral, it went against instinct to let another vampire bite him. That was a damn quick way to end up frothing at the mouth.

Urges tangled in his mind, twisting him up into knots. The desire to bite her was a roiling, living thing in him, but it ran up against the natural instinct to avoid biting and being bitten by another vampire. Atticus had to shake his head hard to clear it as he pressed his weight down on his captive.

Big blue eyes, almost too big for her face, stared up at him.

They looked liquid in the weak pre-dawn light. Her ceremonial makeup was hopelessly smeared. Dust caked her dress and her hair. Her chest heaved, and when she parted her lips to suck in panting breaths, he caught sight of the daintiest, prettiest pair of fangs he'd ever seen in his life.

It wasn't just the run, nor the surge of panic that made his heart pound when he ground out, "I'm not going to hurt you, okay? I'm trying to help you. If you run here, you'll be dead in a few hours. There's no shelter, no caves. No nothing. You'd bake in the sun."

Rather than reply to his very sound argument against running, she wheezed, "Are you my bridegroom or not?"

"No." It pissed him off that she assumed he might be the kind of trash who'd buy a bride. Not that it was fair, knowing what his involvement looked like, but he couldn't help but be a little offended.

Those dark brows drew together, wrinkling the smudged crimson circle painted on her forehead. "Then who are you? You're not— I never saw you in the crypt. You're not an acolyte. I'd remember."

Crypt? A headache pulsed behind his left eye. *So she isn't just dressed up like an acolyte of Grim. She might actually be one. Good gods.*

He'd heard stories of some crypts getting into the extremely lucrative blood bride business, but it was stomach-turning to actually come face to face with it. Atticus wasn't a religious man, but even he felt a little uneasy at the thought of what Grim would think of her own acolytes selling people off to be bred. The goddess was known for her mercy and her celibacy. Somehow he found it hard to believe she'd be down with blood brides, no matter what bullshit the vampiric zealots pushed.

Atticus didn't dare let his captive go, but he did ease a bit of his weight off her when he answered, "I'm your— I was hired to be your driver. I had no idea that you were— that the job was for a blood bride. Fuckin' swear."

She blinked those huge, liquid eyes at him. They looked so innocent. It was hard to believe that this was the same woman who had just tried to beat the shit out of him. "They told me my groom was in California. Are we there already?"

"No." Unease tickled the back of his neck. He glanced up. "C'mon. We need to get back to the RV."

Hauling himself off her, he used his grip on her wrists to leverage her up onto her feet. He realized his mistake almost instantly.

The bride made a low, animal sound of pain as her knees buckled. Too late, he remembered her bloody feet. Crouching to sling one arm behind her knees, he swung her up into his arms with a hissed, "Shit!"

Her eyes were screwed shut and her lips puckered, but she didn't complain as he hustled back the way they'd come. The world was growing dangerously light around them. Some vampires could handle sunlight better than others. Atticus wasn't too sensitive, but he suspected the bride was when she tucked her head into the curve of his neck, hiding her eyes.

His pulse jumped. There was also the possibility that she just wanted to do it. That was a compelling thought.

Or maybe she's just in pain, idiot.

Feeling a little slimy and a lot guilty, Atticus cleared his throat and asked, "You got a name?"

Her breath was hot on his slightly sweaty neck. "Of course I do."

"You gonna give it to me or what?"

"Why do you want to know?"

Good question. It didn't really matter. He was deep in the shit now. It would have been the smart decision to say he wanted to know nothing about her, reducing his liability as much as possible. But he *wanted* to know. And really, there was no chance he was going to be able to put her back in the trailer and forget about her. Whether she gave him her name or not, he was going to help her.

"I'm Atticus," he offered, his voice rougher than normal. That was saying something, too, since his smoke-scarred throat really did a number on his voice. "Atticus Caldwell. You can call me Atty, if you want."

She was quiet as he crossed the last few yards to the RV. He had to nudge her to open the door for him, but eventually they made it safely inside. A good thing, too, since the sun began to crest the horizon not a minute later. Carefully setting her on the bed in the far back, he hunched a bit and moved as fast as he could to pull down the blinds over the windshield and windows, plunging them into comforting darkness.

He stood there for a moment, his hands gripping the head-rests of the driver and passenger seats, trying to collect himself before he faced her again. It wasn't an easy thing when her sweet scent began to fill the small cabin, mixing with the intoxicating tang of real, warm blood.

He'd heard that venom neutral vampires gave off a different scent than normal. Most vampires were repelled, sexually-speaking, by the scent of each other. It was some evolutionary thing. Since they couldn't procreate and could kill one another with a single injection of venom, it made good survival sense to build in a disgust mechanism to one another. There were exceptions, but very few that he knew of.

Frankly, he'd always assumed the venom neutral scent to be a myth. Adriana had never smelled any different to him than another vampire, but she was also his baby sister, so maybe he never stood a chance of noticing that sort of thing.

The bride, though...

If he hadn't seen the bride's fangs or the green, night-glow reflection of her eyes, he would have sworn on every god's name that she was human. Deliciously, potently human.

Atticus tried to breathe through his mouth, but that didn't help. All it did was paint her scent on the back of his tongue, which made the gland in the roof of his mouth pulse and his aching cock begin to leak in his pants. One touch and he'd go off like he was fourteen and getting his cock sucked for the first time again.

There were so many levels to why that was messed up, he couldn't even begin to pick through them all.

He needed to get himself together. He needed to grab his medical kit out of his backpack. He needed—

"Carmine."

Atticus turned his head so fast, the world blurred. "What?"

"That's my name," she explained, nervously smoothing her filthy hair behind her ears. They were just a little too big for her face. *Cute as shit.*

"Do you have a last name, Carmine?" He had a bad feeling knowing her family name wouldn't help him find her people, but he had to ask.

She looked everywhere but him when she answered, "No. It's just Carmine."

"Why?"

"They don't give us names."

And just like that, the arousal that twisted him up so badly disappeared in a puff of smoke. Atticus turned the rest of his body to face her. Speaking slowly, so he didn't let on to the rage that was beginning to rise inside him, he asked, "And why is that?"

Carmine stared down at her battered feet. A grimace flashed across her face for a split second before she locked it down. "Because we're supposed to get new ones anyway."

"When you become your bridegroom's anchor," he finished for her, flat and furious beyond words.

"Yeah."

Atticus squeezed his eyes shut. *I'm going to fucking kill Junger.*

CHAPTER THREE

CARMINE HAD SEEN PLENTY OF MEN IN THE CRYPT. There were dour priests and shifty-eyed acolytes who watched the brides a little too closely. There was the instructor who came to the crypt to help them get their mortician certifications and the quiet, observant healer who'd come around a few times to examine them. A number of her fellow brides were men, too, but they were all kept so isolated from one another that she couldn't say she was familiar with any of them.

But mostly, the men in her life were dead.

She was much more familiar with the shape and scent of them spread out on a slab. Carmine knew the meat of a man — the places where they had hair and she didn't, the sturdiness of their bones, the pliability of their skin as she passed a needle in and out. At first they'd been a marvel, but over time she began to see them as no different than the other bodies that arrived on her table needing care and kindness.

Under the cover of studying for her certification, she'd done other research into the subject — reading that taught her a man was not just the meat he was born in, but could come in infinite variations and identities that went beyond flesh. Knowing these things had helped her understand how to care for the dead better, how to respect them and their identities even when their souls rested by the riverbank, and occupied her mind when she imagined the day her price would be paid.

She thought that when she finally met her bridegroom, she'd be prepared. She wouldn't be shocked by the weight of a man on top of her when the day finally came. Carmine knew exactly how heavy a man could be, how sharp the bristles of their beards sometimes were, and how sometimes they had cocks and sometimes they didn't.

Vague memories of a life before the crypt helped bolster her confidence — not in the direction of her life, but in her ability to understand what would happen next. Unlike most of the brides, she was taken into the crypt late. Carmine had six years in the world before her parents took her to that free clinic for a fever and everything changed.

That was why she never bought the crap that the waxy-faced priest beat into their minds. *Being a blood bride is a life of luxury, a blessing. You will cradle the offspring of Grim herself. You will bring pure life into this world. Your spouses will worship you for the gifts you've—*

Nevermind the fact that Grim was an eternal virgin — something they *loved* to harp on when they spoke of a bride's virtues. Carmine knew that a bridegroom paid a hefty price for a blood bride. She knew that the crypt had been turning a massive profit for years because she'd secretly made friends with one of the administrative workers who loved to gripe about how wealthy they were but how little the office staff was paid.

That money didn't come from donations or funeral services. It came from *them*.

No matter what the acolytes said, anyone who thought to buy another person was bad. She only wanted to live in peace, doing her work with the dead, but a bad man would ruin all of that. Even if he turned out to be the average sort of awful, she knew that her life would never belong to her.

Either she'd die of boredom or wither under the cruel hand of a man who believed he could buy another person. She refused to accept either option.

Carmine had vainly hoped that her bride price would never be paid, that she'd get to live the rest of her life doing what she loved in peace, but then everything went bad all at once.

She overheard the priest cursing the new healer, saying he'd said something to someone. Suddenly there were men with badges at the crypt's doors, asking to speak to all the acolytes, and the head priest's white makeup began to streak with sweat. He managed to send them off, but within days, her fellow blood brides began to disappear, one by one, until only she was left.

It was only a matter of time after that.

She'd thought a thousand times about who would pay her price, what would happen to her, what she'd do if the worst came to pass. Cruel, sweaty faces swam in her mind's eye as she imagined her bridegroom. Someone pasty, with unkempt claws and a sneer. They'd expect her to lay on her back and take the shriveled, wiggly cock between their legs until a baby popped out. The thought made her shudder.

Carmine always knew she'd run, but a part of her was curious to at least see the face of the man who would be her groom. She'd imagined him a thousand different ways as she was dragged out of the crypt, into a van, then a small, beaten m-jet. When the doors to the trailer closed — *stuffy, pitch black even to her vampiric eyes, somewhere she'd been shoved without any warning, would she die there if she was forgotten?* — she expected a cruel face.

What she got was... him. Atticus.

She watched him suspiciously from under her lashes as he puttered around the small RV. There was far more room and amenities in it than the trailer, but he was a very large man. The priests had clucked about her height, saying she was too tall and skinny, but she didn't feel tall when Atticus loomed over her like a thundercloud.

Dressed all in black, he would have blended into the darkness well if it weren't for his pale skin and shock of ginger hair. He was broad-shouldered, slightly stocky, with huge hands and a hard chin. Tattoos peeked out over the collar of his shirt and crawled up his neck. More covered what she'd seen of his hands.

She'd thought she was prepared to deal with men outside of the crypt, but Carmine had never, ever seen a man like him before.

It wasn't just his looks. It was something in how he carried himself that made her skin prickle with a keen sense of danger. Perhaps it was the gun he'd pointed at her that tipped her off, but she thought it was something he carried with him, too. A predatory aura that only her atavistic gray matter could sense.

"Gimme a second," he muttered, like she'd said anything since he began poking around the RV.

Carmine said nothing. She was used to not speaking much. The crypt was a place of silence, and she mostly hung out with the dead, anyway. They weren't great conversationalists, but they were the best listeners.

"Just trying to see if there's a bowl or something— Oh, there we go." Atticus's voice was a deep, raspy baritone. It sounded a bit like someone had taken sandpaper to the inside of his throat. Not in a bad way, exactly, but something about it made her insides squirm.

She watched him pull a plastic bowl out of a cabinet and set it in the sink. He flicked the faucet on. As the bowl filled, he quickly hunted down a towel from another cabinet, set it on the small countertop, and then snagged something from a black backpack by the front seats.

Turning off the water, he lifted the bowl out of the sink and turned to face her. Carmine examined his face unabashedly, fascinated by the hard lines and intense, hooded eyes. It was a very compelling face. Almost as compelling as the rich, clean scent he gave off.

For a moment, he stood there, staring back at her with his lips parted. His tongue darted out, pink and wet, to dab his lower lip. A long, sharp fang caught her eye.

Something crackled down her spine. A jolt of electricity, maybe. Carmine blinked and the moment was broken.

Atticus's pale cheeks went dark with a blush. Her mouth watered, prompting her to wonder when she'd last had a meal. They'd given her a large pack of synth in the trailer, but for once, she didn't have an appetite. Now, though...

He focused his attention on her feet, dangling filthy and bleeding over the edge of the bed. The cuts weren't as bad as they looked, but she knew it was pure luck that she hadn't been hurt worse. There hadn't been time to think of the consequences of running barefoot, though, which was probably why the matron had taken her shoes to begin with.

A deep scowl grooved Atticus's face as he peered at her feet. Carmine fought the urge to shrink away. That look was scary.

He knelt in front of her and set the bowl on the floor. There was hardly room for him to fit there by her feet, but he didn't seem to mind the squeeze as he gently grabbed her ankles and guided her toes to the water.

"Too hot?"

Carmine hadn't been paying attention to anything except him, so it took a second for her to process what he said. When his eyes snapped back up to give her another scowly, impatient look, she shook her head.

"You tell me if you're uncomfortable," he ordered in that gruff, mean voice. It was entirely at odds with how gently he lowered her feet into the warm water. It wasn't even steaming. Just a pleasant, lukewarm temperature. It still stung a little, but not much.

When her feet were fully submerged, he sat back on his haunches and glared up at her from under thick brows. "I need a yes on that, Carmine. It's important."

She blinked at him. "Why?"

For a split second, it looked like the skin of his face was pulled too tight over his skull. His upper lip slid over his fangs and his eyes went hard and dark. "Are you asking me why it's important you acknowledge when I give you an order or are you asking me— Carmine, tell me you're not asking me why it's important that you say so when you're uncomfortable."

Well, how did he expect her to answer? It wasn't the first thing, and he said he didn't want her to tell him the second one, which was the truth, so she settled on silence.

That seemed to be answer enough. Atticus cursed and slapped one of those heavy, tattooed hands over his eyes. "Those mother-fuckers." He took a deep breath and dragged his hand down over his mouth. "Okay. Right. We need to get some shit straight, you and me."

That sounded bad. Carmine watched him warily. He said he wasn't her groom, and she was reasonably confident that whoever that man was, he wouldn't want to receive his bride damaged. Atticus *probably* wouldn't punish her. At least, not in any meaningful way. Maybe he'd take her synth away if she displeased him. That was okay. That happened plenty of times in the crypt. She could go at least a week before it became unbearable.

He watched her feet, those intense eyes following the slow swirl of dirt and blood as the water soaked the filth off. "I'm Atticus. I was hired to transport some cargo into the EVP. I had no idea that it was— that *you* were the cargo. I never would have agreed to it if I did."

Carmine listened carefully, her focus roving around his face. For someone so hard-looking, she thought Atticus was very expressive. He didn't hide behind a thick layer of makeup and he wasn't dead. It was a nice change.

Atticus looked up again, caught her staring, and an expression a little bit like pain crossed his face. His voice came out slightly more strained than before when he said, "I'm gonna ask you some questions, okay? I need you to be honest with me. I can't help you if you're not honest."

Help me? She eyed him up and down. He'd been hired by her groom. Carmine liked the look of him, and might have been able to buy his story that he didn't know what he was doing, but she wasn't stupid enough to trust him.

Nowhere and no *one* was safe. Not for a blood bride.

When she didn't say anything, Atticus pursed his lips. "Why've you gone all quiet?"

"I'm not used to talking," she admitted. "We're not supposed to."

Silence. Obedience. Purity. The three tenets of Grim's blood brides.

A stolen whisper during worship, a quick update from the office staff, answered questions during their lessons — that was about all the brides could expect if they wanted to speak with someone. Mostly, Carmine spoke in her mind. It was always safe to say things there. And to the dead.

Chapter Four

IT WAS A SHOCK TO FEEL ATTICUS'S GENTLE HAND CUP the back of her calf. He gave it a small squeeze when he ground out, "Fuck that. I want to hear you speak with that pretty voice. You don't have to wait for me to ask you a question, but when I do, I expect an answer, okay? That way I can know for sure that you're all right. Do you understand?"

It was instinct to simply nod, but when he raised his eyebrows expectantly, she said, "I understand."

He flashed her a smile. It was all white teeth and soft lips pulled wide and it— There was a *pop!* in her mind, like an old-fashioned light bulb exploding, plunging everything inside her into darkness. Carmine didn't breathe. Didn't dare move. She didn't want to do anything to make that smile go away.

But it did. It faded as he carefully extracted one of her feet from the bowl and began to dab it with a washcloth. "Are you venom neutral?"

"Yes." It seemed like a silly question. Of course she was. No vampire would want her otherwise. In another world, she was born luckier. That Carmine would have potent venom, and she'd never have to worry about being hunted or popping out a groom's offspring on command.

"Figured," Atticus muttered. He stood, fetched and filled another bowl, before he knelt again to begin rinsing her feet. It hurt badly enough that her eyes watered, but she didn't dare make a sound.

"Do you have family, Carmine? Anyone you can call?"

"My family wouldn't answer."

They'd exchanged letters for a while, since brides weren't allowed phones or computer access outside of lessons, but that tapered off when she was still a teen.

His fingers went a little tight on her ankle for a second before they relaxed again. "Why?"

She shrugged. "They knew they couldn't protect me, so they gave me to the crypt. They were paid. They moved on."

Carmine said it without an ounce of bitterness. She didn't blame them for the choice they'd made. A venom neutral child was a blessing and a burden. The big, powerful families used them to make profitable alliances and the poor sold them off to better the lives of the rest of the family.

Even if a family wanted to keep them, it came with considerable risk. It was hard to keep that a secret, and once word was out, the danger that someone could snatch your child and sell them to the highest bidder, or even keep them for themselves until they reached maturity, was very high.

The crypt was the safest option for her parents, who were barely scraping by. She'd be protected there. She'd get an education. She'd be sold to someone who could provide for her when she came of age. It all made sense.

Carmine understood it, but that didn't mean she'd go along with it.

Atticus turned his attention to her other foot. He looked like he was barely listening, but his dark tone said something else. "They wouldn't help you if you asked?"

"That could get them killed. They could never pay the price of my upbringing back, and the crypt would see it as stealing if they didn't."

It didn't matter that she'd worked in the morgue since she was fifteen. They accounted for every penny they'd ever spent on her. Every bottle of synth. Every scrap of clothing. Every drop of water for her showers. All of it went into the bride price.

She didn't want anyone to get hurt on her behalf. Carmine planned to get herself out of this. No one else had to bother themselves.

There were only two ways to escape becoming a blood bride: either she had to run, or she had to defile herself.

Eyeing the vampire carefully drying her feet, she weighed her choices. If she had to pick, she preferred option A. But she'd take option B without a second thought. Sex sounded horrific, but it'd only take one time. She could endure just about anything once.

"I'm gonna make sure there isn't anything trapped in your cuts before I bandage them up." Atticus propped her heel on the thick muscle of his thigh. Snatching a small pen light from what she thought was a first aid kit, he aimed the beam at the sole and began to poke around.

Scowling again, he grabbed some disinfectant swabs. "I don't see anything, but this is still gonna hurt. Sorry."

Carmine curled her dirty fingernails into the blanket under her and bit down on her lips. Her body went rigid as the sting registered. It did hurt. It hurt a *lot*.

But she didn't make a sound. She didn't flinch. If she did, she worried he'd stop making those soft, comforting noises as he worked. Little *shush* sounds and soft *I know, I know, I'm sorry's*. No one had spoken that gently to her in decades.

When he finished her right foot, he smeared what looked like half a tube of disinfectant on the sole before he wrapped it in fancy rubber bandages. There must have been some sort of numbing agent in it, because the pain eased almost immediately.

"You did great," he praised, raspy voice so very gentle. "And that was the worst foot, so you're past the bad part. Once I get the other one wrapped up, let's get you in the shower."

A pang of self-consciousness struck her. Carmine had

forgotten how dirty she was, but all at once she felt the dust caking her skin and hair, the filth clinging to the waxy layer of her makeup. She hated dirt and disorder. Everything needed to be clean, most especially herself.

Without thinking, she asked, "Do I look that bad?"

Atticus went very still. He didn't look at her when he answered, "No. You're beautiful. But you also hauled ass through the desert and then wrestled in the dirt for a while. You need to get clean so you can feel better."

They were quiet for the time it took for him to dress her other foot. Finally, as Atticus stood up to drain the dirty water into the small sink, Carmine worked up the courage to ask, "What happens now?"

"Shower," he grunted. "Then bed."

Back to the trailer, then. Carmine worked hard to keep her face from showing her dismay. The trailer wasn't horrible. It had air conditioning, a tiny bed, a toilet bolted to the wall, and the crate of synth. They'd thrown clothes and toiletries, too, so she didn't show up on her groom's doorstep smelly and disheveled. But that didn't mean she wanted to go back.

Once she was in there, escape was impossible.

It was completely dark inside, and even vampire eyes needed some dim illumination to see with. When she was locked in the trailer, all she could do was listen to her own breathing, wonder if her eyes were truly open or closed, and think of all the ways she could die.

What if I run out of oxygen? What if the trailer is left somewhere? What if no one thinks to see what was inside?

She'd seen bodies baked by the sun, bloated and discolored by undisturbed decay, and much worse. What would she look like on the slab if no one found her in time?

Carmine liked small, dark spaces, but the trailer proved to be too much even for her.

Her gaze slid over Atticus's broad back to eye the door. It

would be stupid to run out into the sunlight. She lived her entire life indoors, so she had absolutely no tolerance for it. He was right that there was no shelter out there. Left to bake in the sun, it'd only take a few hours for her body to shut down, go into shock, and then quit altogether.

But if this was her only chance to escape before he threw her back in the trailer...

A callused hand gripped her jaw. Not hard, but firm enough to turn her head away from the door.

Atticus glowered at her. His thumb curved over the edge of her jaw, stroking through makeup and dirt to reach her skin. "Don't."

Carmine widened her eyes, but said nothing. She was a terrible liar, so she didn't try. Best to just look innocent and hope.

It didn't work. Atticus clearly didn't buy it. "Don't give me those eyes, doll. I know you were thinking of bolting. I'm telling you: *don't.* I'm gonna be pissed if I have to chase you into the sun and haul you back here. That shit could kill you."

And if it did, her groom would be furious. Atticus would be in trouble for letting such a huge investment die such a stupid death.

He's going to get in trouble no matter what, she tried to reason with herself. *I'm not going to my groom. What does it matter?*

She really didn't want to die, but could she risk there never being another chance to bolt? What if he locked her back in the trailer and never opened the doors again?

Panic clawed at her throat and shoved words out of her mouth before she could check them. "Will I be let out again?"

Atticus's brows furrowed. "Let out of where?"

Carmine squeezed her hands together in her lap so hard, she could feel her bones move. "The trailer."

His face cleared, then went stormy again. He crouched low, bringing them eye to eye, and released her jaw in favor of brushing her hair back behind her ears. He was so, so close. Too close.

Carmine fixed her gaze on what looked like the barrel of a tattooed gun peeking out from beneath his shirt's collar.

"Doll, look at me."

She was too used to following commands. It was a habit to listen.

He held her gaze, unblinking, when he promised, "I'm not putting you back in that fucking trailer. No one is. You're safe with me. You're gonna sleep in this bed today and then tonight we'll figure everything out. Understand?"

She nodded.

"Words, doll."

Carmine uncurled her lips from where she'd tucked them between her teeth. "I understand?"

A corner of his mouth kicked up. "That didn't sound very convincing."

She could feel the heat of her flush and hoped what remained of her makeup hid it from his too-intense eyes. "I'm a bad liar."

"Yeah? I like that about you." Tilting his head toward the narrow door at the far end of the kitchen area, he ordered, "Shower."

Atticus stood up slowly. She immediately missed the heat of his body so close to her. Clearly, it'd been too long since she had a meal. Her body temperature had obviously plummeted, and that was why she wanted to press her face into his chest and just soak in all that gorgeous warmth.

She looked down at her dress and wrinkled her nose. "My clothes are in the trailer."

He shook his head and turned to rummage in his backpack again. After a moment, he extracted what looked like a blanket. It was only when he passed it to her that she realized it was a massive, well-worn t-shirt.

His voice got impossibly raspier when he muttered, "That should hold you over until tomorrow." He walked over to the bathroom, and since he wasn't looking at her, she risked a quick sniff of the shirt.

Her toes curled with delight even as the roof of her mouth began to ache. *Mm,* she thought, watching him open the door to reveal the world's smallest shower stall and toilet. Her stomach rumbled. *He smells delicious.*

CHAPTER FIVE

THE SHIRT CAME DOWN TO HER KNEES AND SHE STILL
felt more naked than she ever had before.

Carmine peeked out of the door warily, her face already hot.
Her heart pounded within her ribcage. Atticus was impossible to
miss in the small space. He sat on one of the low benches that
framed the comically small table at the foot of the bed. His broad
shoulders were hunched, his long coat removed. There were straps
over his shoulders. It took her a second to realize he wore a gun
holster. He'd pushed the sleeves of his shirt up, revealing a fasci-
nating array of vampiric skulls and thorny vines and flowers
sprayed over thick, sturdy forearms.

Atticus looked up from his phone the moment her gaze
landed on him. He went preternaturally still.

Her fingers tightened around the small latch that acted as a
doorknob. The heat of her blush could have rivaled the sun. She
couldn't remember the last time someone had seen her without
her makeup or her veil.

Grim's acolytes painted themselves and veiled their heads in a
commitment to modesty and selflessness. All genders wore long
white gowns. Jewelry, haircuts, and tattoos were forbidden. Brides

especially weren't allowed to alter their bodies in any way that wasn't pre-approved by the matron in charge of their care.

That was why she'd had her body hair lasered off, but she'd never had more than the dead ends carefully trimmed from her head. She painted her face and hands, but she couldn't dream of a tattoo or even glittery eyeshadow. She wore her gowns, but never dared to ask if she might try a color other than white.

One reason so many brides looked forward to their bride price being paid was the relative freedom it came with. The matron liked to remind them all the time that if they were chosen, they could dress however their spouses liked. They might get to own a pair of sneakers, or lip gloss, or even cut their hair.

Carmine longed to try those things, but she didn't account for how nude she would feel without her costume, the mask she'd worn for so long.

And the way Atticus looked at her... it definitely felt like she was nude.

He said something too low for her to hear, pressed his thumb and forefinger into his eyes, and then muttered, "That was fast. Was everything okay? Do you need something?"

The bathroom had been fully stocked. The soaps and things weren't quite as good of a quality as she was used to — a bride *must* have soft skin — but everything was there. In fact, she'd taken the luxury of a whole extra minute in the shower, just to see if she could.

"I'm okay," she answered, because he kept waiting for her to say something.

Atticus dropped his hand and fixed her with a *look*. "Why'd you go so fast? You didn't have to hurry. My sister takes *ages* in the shower. She says it's a woman's right."

He has a sister? Yes, that seemed right. She didn't know what it was like having siblings, but she thought she could see Atticus fitting into a big brother mold very easily.

Must be nice to have someone looking out for you.

"I took an extra minute," she reminded him as she shuffled her way out of the bathroom. There were really only a few feet between the bathroom and the bed, but the journey felt like it took ages. Probably because Atticus watched her so closely.

"Extra minute?"

Carmine tried very hard not to look guilty. "Yes. I was in the shower for five minutes. Didn't you notice?"

He seemed distracted. His eyes kept darting down to the shirt she'd borrowed, then back up, like he was trying not to look and failing. Maybe that was why it took him a second to ask, "What are you talking about?"

She wasn't sure where she was supposed to sleep or even sit, but there wasn't exactly a bevy of options, so she settled back on the edge of the bed and tucked her bare legs under her. Carefully arranging her long rope of wet hair over her shoulder, she began to braid it so it would be more manageable.

"In the crypt, we're only allowed four minutes of shower time. Two minutes of water with a minute break in between."

Atticus looked at her like she'd just plucked something from inside a corpse and waved it around. "Why would they do that?"

"Longer showers encourage vanity and sloth," she replied, by rote. After a heartbeat, she took a risk by adding, "Also, I think they didn't want us to be alone together for any longer than that. The showers were communal and they couldn't risk any of us being defiled."

A couple tried it once and things went very, very badly for them. Personally, Carmine didn't understand the appeal. It was a good way to get out of being a bride, certainly, but only if you succeeded. If you didn't, the punishment would be endless. Not to mention the fact that the act itself seemed awful.

Atticus's expression didn't ease up. If anything, he looked more disgusted than when she started.

"Okay, new rule," he rumbled, standing up slowly from his seat. He planted his hands on the tiny tabletop and a muscle in his jaw ticced. "No more five minute showers."

Her stomach sank, but before it could go too far, he continued, "You take as long as you fucking want. Ten minutes. Twenty. Fuck, an *hour* if that's what you need. Look at all that hair. No way five minutes is enough. There's a fancy water recycler in this thing, so take as long as you need to."

Ten-minute showers? Her stomach exploded with excited butterflies. She hadn't experienced a luxury like that since she was little and her mother used to give her baths in the plastic tub of their one-bedroom apartment.

"And another thing— This isn't the crypt anymore. You don't have to ask me permission for shit. You don't have to watch what you say. You can't run because you could get hurt, but everything else... You're your own person. All that stuff was bullshit, okay? Whoever taught you that— that shit about *defilement* was a piece of garbage and if they were here, I'd shoot them."

Carmine was only halfway done with her braid, but her fingers refused to move. She could only stare, wide-eyed, as Atticus stalked over to his backpack and snatched it up. He looked so angry, but it wasn't directed at her. She felt it, though, like a furnace getting hotter and hotter.

It was on the tip of her tongue to ask why he was making rules for her if she wasn't supposed to ask for permission for things, but she didn't. Instead, she found herself saying, "My groom might not like that."

He stopped by the bed and turned his head to lash her with a glare. "What part?"

"Any of it." She licked her lips and looked away, afraid that if she held his gaze for a moment longer, she'd catch fire. "I'm not supposed to listen to anyone but my groom. If he wants—"

A tug on the loose end of her braid stopped her mid-sentence. Atticus held the dripping ends of her hair in his tattooed fist, but he didn't yank it. He wrapped it once, twice, around his knuckles before he gently pulled her head back, forcing her to meet his gaze.

He looked much calmer when he told her, "Your groom is a dead man, doll. Stop thinking about him."

Her heart leapt, but Carmine knew better than to hope, to trust. If anything, the cold look in Atticus's eyes made her more afraid. She thought she understood how to deal with a man who'd pay her bride price, but *him?* There was no telling what he wanted from her, let alone what he'd do next.

She couldn't rely on him to save her. For all she knew, he was worse than her groom. He could kidnap her, sell her to someone else. Offer her as a broodmare to other vampires. Take her for himself.

It was the oddest thing, the physical reaction she had to that last thought. A flush rolled down from her chest to her toes, and something warm unfurled in the lowest part of her stomach.

Atticus slowly unwound her hair from around his knuckles. When he was done, he skimmed them over her clothed shoulder. That warmth in her stomach grew hotter, bigger, and oddly a little heavier.

Maybe he saw the panic in her eyes. Maybe he understood that a bride couldn't trust anyone — especially those who claimed to want to help. Whatever the reason, his expression went from terrifying to soft in a heartbeat.

"Easy, doll. I'm not going to let anyone touch you, okay?" He gave her shoulder a gentle nudge. Carmine didn't understand what he wanted her to do until her back hit the mattress. Using one hand, he pulled the blankets out from under her and draped them over her legs. He gave the top of her bandaged foot a gentle pat. "Sleep. I'm gonna shower."

"Okay." She tracked him as he moved toward the bathroom.

Opening the door, he reminded her, "No running. If you do, I'll hunt you down, and you're not gonna like what I'll have to say when I catch you. Got it?" He cast her one of those stern looks over his shoulder, demanding a response.

Carmine hid the lower half of her face beneath a sheet and curled on her side, her eyes glued to the wide shape of his back, his sturdy waist, the funny way the short bristles of hair on the nape of his neck came together in a triangular shape. Her voice came out whispery when she answered, "Got it."

And just like that, he gifted her another one of those brilliant smiles. "Thatta girl."

Chapter Six

He could feel her eyes on him. They were like soft little hands ghosting over his skin, leaving him tense and breathless with every glancing touch. It was a struggle to continue breathing deeply, evenly, as if he were asleep. Her scent coated his tongue and throat. He'd spent half the day trying to categorize it and the other half lightly dozing, afraid that if he slipped into a deep sleep he'd wake up to find her gone.

Cherry.

That was the scent. He'd never had one before, since he was a born vampire and never had the sick urge to put that shit in his mouth, but he'd smelled them. It wasn't the kind that looked radioactive, but the dark, bloody cherries he saw floating in black syrup a time or two. Rich and sweet but complex, almost too ripe.

It made him *wild.*

But not half as wild as the thought of her watching him from the bed with those big eyes, as she slowly peeled the covers back. She'd have to step over him, since he'd slept on the narrow strip of floor wedged between the bed and the kitchenette, with only a blanket and a stiff pillow for comfort. Not a moment later the softest sound of her bandaged feet touching the floor by his hip was barely discernible over the low hum of the heating unit.

He was so attuned to her, he could feel the air move when she carefully crept over him. All of his focus was on her — too much, perhaps, because it took him an embarrassingly long time to see the bigger picture and realize she was headed for his gun.

She didn't make it more than two steps before he jackknifed up into a sitting position and fisted the back of her shirt.

Carmine gasped and stumbled over his legs. Made clumsy by the thick, rubbery bandages on her feet, she went down easy. Atticus caught her around the waist and settled her across his lap. It all happened in less than a handful of seconds, but he saw it unfold slowly. He could feel and hear every one of his heart beats. He watched her turn her head to fix him with a hunted, guilty look. He was fascinated by the silky expanse of her legs as they tangled, went down, and then stretched over his lap.

And then time caught up to him in the same instant as his temper.

His voice was grittier than normal for multiple reasons when he growled, "What did I say, doll?"

She didn't reply. Carmine sat as still and stiff as a statue in his arms, but her eyes were huge, full of life in that heart-stopping face.

Obviously, she was striking in her ceremonial makeup, but without it... Atticus's fingers twitched with the urge to smooth the pads over her bare cheeks. Her skin wasn't the chalky white he assumed it was. It was a rich golden color that paired perfectly with her raven's wing hair and wide eyes. He guessed her ancestry traced back somewhere to northern Africa or the middle east, but with vampires it was impossible to say for sure.

The vampiric gene pool was a kaleidoscope by necessity. They hailed from all corners of the world and weren't picky about mates, so long as the urges to feed and breed were satisfied. For vampires, it was all about prestige. Power. Being the protector or the protected. It was about the strength and ruthlessness of one's line. How far back could you trace it? How long had you survived a world that was so hostile to their kind?

It was so very easy for a vampire's line to die out. Breeding was incredibly involved and difficult, not to mention the fact that they lived dangerous lives rife with vendettas and violence. If breeding failed, one could turn a vampire and they would be considered an heir, but turning had an abysmal success rate.

All it would take was one bad generation and *poof!* A whole bloodline could vanish.

Atticus doubted Carmine came from a notable bloodline, though. A family who sold her to a crypt was probably about as well off as his own parents were. Not that he cared. His father was a turned vampire sired by another, anonymous turned vampire, which meant his bloodline was a mess and too new to mean anything anyway. He wouldn't have put stock in that shit even if came from some hoity-toity family, but it was a relief to know he wouldn't be bringing down the wrath of an old, distinguished line on his head by rescuing Carmine.

Not that being from an unknown line would save her from being coveted, obviously. It wouldn't matter if she emerged from the gooey center of a landfill, fully formed and stinking. Carmine was a vampire who could carry vampiric offspring. For some folks, that was more valuable than even the most prestigious family name.

And she tried to run off. *Again.*

He knew he shouldn't be mad. Carmine didn't know him, had absolutely no reason to trust him, and in her position, he'd do the same. But logic didn't take away the vice of fear that squeezed his heart when he imagined her out there in the desert, wandering barefoot until she hit a road. He didn't even care that she'd been headed for his gun, probably so she could negotiate her way out of the situation or simply to have some protection when she fled.

He cared that she would have been hurt.

"What was the plan?" he demanded, jabbing a finger in the direction of the door. He knew he was using his *scary big brother voice,* as Adriana liked to say, but he couldn't stop it. "Were you gonna run out into the desert and hitchhike your way to the nearest town? Maybe put that gun to my head and tell me to let you go? Gods, Carmine, do you have any idea what could happen to you out there? What could happen if you misfired a bolt gun?"

His skin crawled. It was like fire ants had replaced the blood in his veins. *Carmine in a stranger's car, no money, no phone, no one to help her. Carmine lost in the desert as sunrise approaches. Carmine being chased down by that pack of coyotes, her bare feet shredded by the rough ground. Carmine stumbling across an unexploded bomb left by the war. One wrong step and— gone.*

Still, she said nothing. Her expression was rigid, but her eyes were so big, so bright and wary. He couldn't decide if he wanted to crush her to his chest or channel Harlan and give her a scolding so blistering, she'd never fucking forget it.

He nearly gave in to the impulse to do one or the other, but managed to restrain himself at the last second. *I'm scaring her. Fuck. I know better than that.*

His sister was so, so sensitive growing up. All it took was a single annoyed look and she'd burst into tears, run off, and find some small place to hide until he or Harlan coaxed her out again. He knew better than to let his temper get the better of him.

Forcing himself to swallow the lump of fear in his throat, he let out a slow breath. "I'm sorry. I shouldn't have— You scared me and I reacted badly."

Her expression didn't change one iota. It was like she was bracing herself for something. More anger? Atticus skimmed his hand up her spine and was a little startled to feel the bumps — not just of her vertebrae, but her ribs, too. *Did they not fucking feed her?*

Venom neutral vampires who didn't get the right nutrition could easily get underweight. Bad synth and irregular feeding could snowball and become devastating. Vampires were already at a disadvantage, since their diet was so lean in fat, but venom neutral vampires were even more at risk. They couldn't miss out on anything. And now that he was really paying attention, he thought her body temperature was low, too. That was a bad sign.

Still, she said nothing. She wouldn't stop staring at him. It drove him a little crazy.

"Hey," he muttered, at a loss. Atticus knew he didn't have the right, but she was so stiff, so cold, and his words didn't seem to be doing much, so he cupped the side of her head and gently coaxed her to lean into him.

His lust hadn't gone away. His cock was hard behind his fly, his blood was hot, and her sweet cherry scent made the roots of his fangs ache like a motherfucker, but none of that mattered so he ignored it. He could make out the erratic beat of her heart. The sound made some unknown organ in his chest go so tight, it squeezed the breath out of him.

"I'm sorry. I understand why you feel like you need to run. I get it. I really, *really* do. But you scared me and that made me upset. I'm not angry at you, okay? You're not in trouble."

It'd been a long damn time since he held a woman this way. He'd forgotten how much he liked it until soft fingers fiddled with a fold of his shirt and warm breath tickled his ear.

Stroking his fingers through her hair, he continued, "I just need you to understand what could have happened. Even if you'd gotten away, even if you'd gotten my gun — *big* if — there's nothing within a hundred miles of us right now. You probably would have gotten turned around in the desert. You might have hit another road, but any kind of person could have picked you up. It's not safe, doll."

He didn't expect her to speak. He loved the sound of her soft soprano voice, but he'd quickly picked up that she used her eyes to do the real talking. When she was really unsure, she kept that pretty voice locked away.

It felt like a bit of a gift when she said, in a surprisingly frank tone, "It's dark now."

"Yeah, but it won't be forever. Do you think you could walk a hundred miles in one night? And do you even know how to shoot a gun?"

There was a thoughtful pause, then an almost imperceptible sigh. "No."

"Right."

She lapsed into silence, her chin jutting at a stubborn angle. He liked that tiny, almost imperceptible hint of sass. It reminded him that though she might look like a doll, she was the same woman who'd fought like a wild thing in the dirt and didn't hesitate to go for his gun when she had the chance.

Atticus knew he had to move. She needed to drink — a painful pulse in the roof of his mouth reminded him that they *both* needed to drink — and he needed to figure out what they were going to do. Junger would die, obviously, but his first priority was getting Carmine squared away. She had to be somewhere safe, with people he could trust to look after her.

A deep, dark wave of feeling washed through him, churning his insides until everything felt raw and unfamiliar. *Can I trust anyone?*

His arm tightened around her middle. The thought of leaving her alone with anyone but him made the tendons of his neck strain against his skin. He hated the idea. If something happened to her when he wasn't around, he'd...

What?

Atticus gave himself a hard internal shake. He had to get a grip. This whole thing had fucked with his head and he wasn't thinking clearly.

I need to call the boss.

He hated to involve Harlan, but his father would know what to do. He'd make the right call. He always did.

The thought made him feel better. Atticus could handle himself, but he didn't have to. Harlan and the rest of the men who'd followed him out of syndicate life would have his back.

And now they'd have Carmine's, too, even if she didn't know it.

CHAPTER SEVEN

CARMINE PERCHED LIKE A BIRD IN THE PASSENGER'S seat, a bottle of synthblood clutched in her hands, and dressed in another simple white gown she'd pulled out of a cardboard box in the trailer. Luckily they'd found a paper-thin pair of slippers in there, too, so she no longer hopped around on just her bandages.

They'd been driving for a couple hours. Every few minutes, she'd shoot him a look out of the corner of her eye, then take a sip of her drink. She didn't look like she enjoyed it much.

He could empathize. There must have been something off with the batch, because he normally enjoyed the brand stocked in the RV. But the bottle he'd forced himself to polish off before they set out tasted like chemicals, all hard metal and salt. There wasn't a bit of sweetness to it, and that bothered him for some reason.

When they made a pit stop, he'd get a different brand for them. In the meantime, he kept his displeasure to himself, since he didn't want to say anything that would discourage her from finishing her meal.

"Where are we going?"

He wondered if the sound of her voice would always be a bit of a shock. Every time she spoke, his body responded in visceral and deeply inappropriate ways.

"We're headed to California," he answered, gruffer than she deserved.

"So you *are* taking me to my groom." Carmine didn't sound hurt by that. If anything, she seemed to expect it.

The muscles bracketing his jaw tensed reflexively. "No," he bit out. "And I told you to stop thinking about him."

"Well, if it's not the man who paid my bride price, then it's someone else."

At this rate, he was going to crack a damn molar. "No, it's not."

"Someone is going to try to be my groom," she very reasonably pointed out.

"That someone is a dead man," he replied, equally reasonable. "All the someones are dead men. Now, stop thinking about grooms and shit. Seriously, you're not allowed to worry about that anymore. That's a rule."

"How come you're allowed to tell me what to do? Are *you* going to be my groom?"

"Fuck no." He didn't mean to spit the words out, but he couldn't contain them. The idea that he might take a blood bride when he'd spent most of his life protecting Adriana from that fate was repulsive.

There was a wide, wide gulf between taking a *blood bride* and taking an anchor, a mate. One was a disgusting institution based on antiquated ideals of bloodline purity and the other was sacred. A partnership. He'd never considered taking a vampiric anchor before, but he wasn't put off by the idea itself, only the idea that he might want one for the same reason Junger did.

Carmine didn't look at him. Before, she'd done it regularly, about every two minutes, but now she seemed intent on watching the road. "If you're not my groom, and you're not delivering me to the one who paid my bride price, *and* you're not going to sell me to someone else, why are we going to California?"

A fair question.

"Because that's where we're expected to go. This RV is being tracked. Junger trusts me to do the job, but he'd be an idiot to trust me *completely*. If I deviate from the course too much, he's gonna send someone after us." Atticus rolled his shoulders back, trying to ease the sudden knot of tension between the blades. He could handle anyone Junger sent, but the risk it would pose to Carmine was intolerable.

"Junger?"

"The dead man," he growled.

"I don't understand. You're delivering me to him but you're not?"

Oh, she was starting to get annoyed with him. Atticus slid her a quick look and found her jaw firmly set. Those big eyes were narrowed at the road and her lips, soft and plush, were pursed.

He didn't like upsetting her, but he *did* feel an odd sort of thrill at the tart note in her voice. Atticus had to resist the urge to flatten his tongue against the roof of his mouth, easing the ache in his venom gland, when he replied, "I live in California, dollface."

"So?"

"So, I'm taking you home with me, where I know you'll be safe." He watched her out of the corner of his eye and held his breath. There was no reason for him to be so invested in her response, but there he was.

Of course she didn't immediately sigh with relief and bat those long, curly lashes at him. Instead, her shoulders went stiff and the look she sent his way was one of the deepest suspicion.

She said nothing, but he swore he could hear her thoughts hollering at him. Carmine didn't believe a single word out of his mouth.

Smart, but irritating.

Clearing his throat, Atticus took one hand off the wheel to fish his phone out of his pocket. Normally he'd never call Harlan during a job, just for security's sake, but this was going to have to be an exception.

Clipping the phone into the holder on the dashboard, he checked the time before pulling up the boss's contact card.

Harlan never used to sleep in, but having an anchor and a daughter had thankfully mellowed him out a bit. Now he actually slept in a few hours past sundown and occasionally did fun shit. *A miracle.*

The phone rang twice before Harlan picked up. Atticus glanced at his passenger before flicking the button to connect the phone to the RV's sound system.

"Atticus. Tell me what you need."

Carmine jolted in her seat. He wasn't sure if it was the volume or the surprise of hearing another man's voice that startled her, but he didn't like it. Reaching over the center console to settle his hand on her raised knee, he answered, "I've got a problem, boss."

"What kind?"

"The kind where we're gonna have to dig a deep hole."

There was a pause. "Junger."

"Yup." Atticus rubbed circles over her kneecap with his thumb, mostly to calm himself down. Every time he thought of the man, it was like a firecracker of pure rage exploded in his chest. "It wasn't cargo he had me pick up. Fucker bought a bride."

Harlan didn't waste time getting mad or asking dumb questions. His trust in Atticus was absolute. There were no uncertainties, no worry that Atticus might not grasp the situation or be misinformed. They'd worked together and been family too long for that.

"Is she with you?"

"She's listening right now." He felt Carmine tense and gave her knee a reassuring squeeze. "Her name's Carmine and she needs somewhere safe to go. You cool with me bringing her to the estate?"

"Of course," Harlan answered, entirely unfazed by the idea that Atticus might be bringing trouble home. "Carmine, it's a pleasure to meet you. My name is Harlan Bounds. You're welcome to stay with us for however long you need. My anchor will be ecstatic to have you as a neighbor. Atticus, I'll have one of the cottages cleared out for her. Medical care is on call if necessary when you arrive."

That new thing in his chest went tight and mean all of a sudden. It was like a leg cramp, but one that made him want to snarl into the phone, *"Absolutely fucking not."*

He had his own house on Empire Estate, the large swath of land that Harlan purchased when they hightailed it out of the New Zone. It'd once been a thriving gold mine. The property was home to a manor and about a dozen homes scattered in a circle all around the farthest edge, off the beaten path from the manor and its attached gardens. Most of them were vacant. Harlan's security team, led by Atticus, had all claimed one of the stone cottages, but they lived in the guard house by the gate during their shifts. Technically, a cottage belonged to Adriana, too, but she preferred to stay in the manor when she visited.

There were four cottages still unoccupied. They were all modernized and cleaned up when Harlan bought the place. Carmine would be totally comfortable in one. There were exactly zero reasons for him to be pissed about the idea that she wouldn't be staying with him instead.

Why didn't I think of that? It hadn't even occurred to him. He'd just assumed she'd come stay in his house. That way he could keep an eye on her. That seemed reasonable.

Except he knew it wasn't. Empire Estate was locked up tighter than an elvish prison, especially after the scare they'd had when Zia was kidnapped. And now that Harlan and Zia were on their way to having a big, happy family? Junger would have to find an army if he wanted to so much as peek over the fence.

Carmine didn't need to be right under his nose to be safe, and arguing the point would only raise a lot of questions he was in no state of mind to answer.

Luckily, he didn't have to figure out what to say right away. Carmine beat him to it.

In her high, no nonsense voice, she asked, "Are you going to sell me, Mr. Bounds?"

Atticus choked on nothing, but Harlan was as unflappable as ever. "No. I'd like to help you. And call me Harlan."

"Why? You don't know me."

"I don't, but Atticus does. That's all I need."

"Why does he call you boss?"

"Habit. He started calling me that when we met. He was thirteen and too scared to use my first name, so it was boss or Mr. Bounds. Then he preferred it to dad. And I *am* still his boss, though you wouldn't know it by how he acts."

Carmine's lips popped open with surprise. "You're his dad?"

Atticus drummed his claws against the steering wheel. He didn't normally tell strangers anything about his past — not even the few potential anchors he'd gone out with — and Harlan was even less inclined toward sharing. But a woman who'd been bought and sold again as a blood bride couldn't trust anyone, so a little sharing was necessary. If they wanted to establish trust, then they had to show a little, too.

Harlan wasn't a particularly verbose man and he generally didn't need to be. His word was law. When he said jump, you did it. Not because he was scary, but because he'd earned the respect of his people over and over.

Zia'd softened him up a bit, though, and it showed when he patiently explained, "I adopted Atticus and his sister when they were kids. We're family. I trust him to know what's right. If he says you need help, then you've got it."

"Oh." Carmine looked lost. That new organ in his chest spasmed again.

Always good at reading people, Harlan switched the conversation back to Atticus. "Tell me the plan, boy. You want me to call your sister? She'll want to meet Carmine."

"That's a good idea. Ask her if she's comfortable staying a few days." He wouldn't disclose her secret to anyone, not even Carmine, but if she wanted to come and reveal that she was also a venom neutral vampire, Atticus figured it would help things along. Adriana could relate to Carmine, at least a little bit, and hopefully help her adjust.

"Junger expects me back in Sacramento in about a week. I figure I head back like he expects, but I meet up with one of our men a day before. Send Michael out. He can pick her up and drive all day back home. I'll drop off the trailer at the spot, handle Junger, and then head back."

"I can handle him for you."

It was a humbling offer, considering Harlan was one of the most feared assassins in the UTA, but Atticus shook his head. "Zia'd be mad."

"Not if I told her why. She's got a mean streak a mile wide when you get her righteousness going."

The estate's former rosarian, Zia was all sunshine and roses and sweet smiles, but she was also the witch who shoved her own poisoned blood down a vampire's throat with zero hesitation. She didn't want Harlan doing any murder for hire, but if he did it to protect someone, Atticus was pretty sure she wouldn't be too upset. But they had a kid now, and that meant the stakes were different. Even though he was certain Harlan would never be caught, he couldn't allow him to take the risk.

And even if I could...

"Thanks, but I'm gonna pass." He didn't turn his head to see Carmine's expression, but he felt her eyes on him when he added, "I want to kill the sonuvabitch myself."

CHAPTER EIGHT

IT WAS LATE, CARMINE WAS TIRED, HUNGRY, AND growing increasingly uneasy.

They'd pulled over at a dusty pit stop. Sunrise was coming, and Atticus said he wanted to pick up a different synth brand before they found a safe place to park for the day.

She appreciated that for a few reasons: first, she hated the taste of the synth they had earlier in the night, and second, he'd given her another chance to run.

A part of her didn't want to. That part was weak and tired. It wanted her to believe everything Atticus said, everything Harlan assured her was true, but it was so outlandish that she couldn't. What were the odds that she'd get that lucky? They wanted to offer her a free place to stay *and* take care of her groom? If she could have believed it, Carmine would have wept with relief.

But good things like that didn't happen to people. At least, not to blood brides. And if she took the risk, then she'd be putting her life in unknown hands. Sure, Atticus seemed nice — growly, short-tempered, oddly compelling — but that could all be an act. He could smile at her one minute and then the next she'd find herself locked in a different cage.

She didn't want to be locked in a cage. Not even a nice one. Carmine wanted to have her own life. She wanted to cut her hair. She wanted to find a job in a funeral home and do what she loved. She wanted to have her own money and in her own time find a real anchor, not just a groom, who wouldn't expect her to give and receive nothing in return.

So as much as she longed to stay with Atticus, breathing in his delicious scent and listening to that strange, smoky voice, she knew that it was impossible.

"Do you need any products or anything?" Atticus pointed out the aisle to her left, where a sea of things she only barely recognized were lined up neatly on white metal shelves. It'd been so long since she'd been in a store, but her eyes immediately jumped to the makeup section. It looked relatively unchanged from when she used to go shopping with her mother at the dime store.

Her eyes stung. The urge to run over and inspect the small eyeshadow palettes was a beast in her chest. She wanted to move so fast her thin slippers flew right off her bandaged feet.

But she had no money, and she wasn't about to ask Atticus to pay for things she didn't need. Not when she was leaving, and not when it might all go into some debt she'd have to repay later.

Carmine shook her head and averted her eyes from the glossy labels, perfume bottles, and eyelash curlers.

Atticus touched her back. He did that a lot, and every time it sent a flurry of butterflies through her stomach like a sweet storm. "You sure, doll? No lotions? Nail polish? Lipstick? What about some ties for your hair?"

Yes, she wanted to shout. *Yes, I want all of those things!* But she shook her head again. Afraid he'd see her longing and that her willpower wouldn't outlast him, she announced, "I have to use the restroom."

She could hear the frown in his voice when he replied, "There's a bathroom in the RV. Let's get our stuff and head back."

Daring to meet his gaze, she resisted the light push of his hand on her back. "It doesn't have much privacy. I want to use the one here." When he still looked like he was going to argue, she widened her eyes and added, "Please, Atticus. I won't be long."

He clearly didn't like it. She could see he wanted to tell her no, but after several seconds of scowling, he sighed and guided her in the opposite direction of the register. "Fine. You take as long as you need. I'll be right out here."

Carmine nodded and tried not to look guilty as she passed him. He leaned against the wall, the case of synth he'd picked up set by his booted feet, and crossed his bulky arms. Nothing in his posture screamed that he knew what she was doing, but she also hadn't been able to tell he was awake when she tried to grab his gun at dusk, either.

Not her smartest plan, that. She should have just bolted for the door and taken her chances, but howling animals had woken her and made her think it would be smart to steal his weapon.

Stupid. Animals are way less dangerous than men. Now I have to find another way to escape.

Escape, option A, was still the most preferable of the two available to her. Option B seemed daunting before she'd met Atticus, but now that she had... Her stomach flipped at the thought of those rough hands on her intimate places. Sex had never sounded *good* to her, but when she imagined doing it with him, there was a different sort of feeling that engulfed her.

It was a bit like the desire to stick one's hand in a fire. Just once. Just to know what it felt like, even if it hurt.

But Carmine hadn't come this far to get burned.

He didn't stop her from entering the single occupant bathroom. He didn't knock on the door when she flipped the lock. Her nerves jangled as she scanned the room. Reluctance made her slow. Gods, she wanted what Atticus promised her — the gentle touches, the smiles, the little house, the safety.

She didn't want to crawl out of the tiny, grimy window above the toilet. She didn't want to run into the night and be completely on her own. Sure, she was educated. She had skills in childcare, budgeting, household management, and a mortician's certification. But Carmine had no experience in the real world, no contacts, no *money*. She hadn't lived long outside of the crypt, but she remembered that much about the outside world: it ran on cash.

But staying wasn't an option. She couldn't put her fate into Atticus's hands.

Carmine hiked her long white skirt around her knees and climbed onto the toilet. Her hands were sweaty and the latch on the window was rusty. It took four tries to open it, and one time she used so much force that she nearly threw herself off the toilet.

Flushed with exertion and knowing she was running out of time, she scrambled onto the tank and braced her palms on the metal window frame. It was thin and cut into her palms, but she forced herself up and out.

Her skirt caught on something, audibly tearing the thick white fabric, and several pieces of hair were ripped from the root, but she managed to wiggle her way out of the tiny window. Unfortunately, she didn't think to calculate how far she'd be from the ground when she came out the other side.

Carmine swallowed a scream as she pitched herself out. The dusty, cracked concrete rose up to greet her as she flailed for something to hold on to. But momentum wasn't on her side, and there was no stopping the unfortunate meeting of her face and the ground.

At the last second, she closed her eyes and threw out her hands, hoping to at least spare herself a little damage.

The breath exploded out of her as her middle connected with something hard. A band of steel closed over the back of her legs and she experienced the oddest sensation of being suspended even higher above the ground than she was a second ago.

"Nice try, scamp," Atticus rumbled beneath her. The sound

of a plastic bag rustling came a moment before they began to sway with his long strides. "I should've probably told you before, but I'm pretty experienced with this stuff. Escaping through the bathroom window isn't gonna cut it with me. Especially when you have the world's worst poker face."

Carmine opened her eyes to find Atticus's back and tight, round backside staring up at her. He carried a plastic bag with one hand. It swayed in and out of view as he strolled back to the RV.

He had time to buy the synth?

A humiliated flush crawled up her neck and settled into her cheeks. "Let me go!"

"Not happening, doll." She jolted at the feeling of his skin on her thigh when his thumb happened to find the tear in her dress.

Atticus's step faltered. His thumb pressed a little more firmly into her flesh. "What's this? Did you hurt yourself?"

"No," she replied, mutinous.

He took a deep breath. "Good. Don't do that shit again."

"I can't stay with you!"

"Why not?"

She wasn't sure if it was all the blood pooling in her head or his tone that made her want to hit him, but she did. Not that it made a difference. Her fist bounced off his muscled back like it was made of rubber.

"Because," she snapped, trying again. *Smack! Smack! Smack!* "I don't *trust* you!"

"I'm picking up on that, yeah." Atticus came to a stop by the edge of the parking lot. He dropped the bag on the ground, rummaged in his pocket for a second, and then something beeped. A moment later, she was upright again, swaying in the passenger's seat.

Bracing his hands on the top of the vehicle, he stretched in front of her — all muscle and predatory grace. He filled the entire doorway, glowering at her with those heavy brows and intense eyes. "Listen, dollface, I understand how scary this is for you, and you're damn smart not to trust anyone. Someday soon I hope you'll see I'm one of the few folks who'll never hurt a hair on your head. Until then, you've gotta get this straight — you are *never* going to escape me, okay? Never. I'm a professional. I'm a hunter. I'm a bad motherfucker who's done shit that'd turn all your pretty hair gray. I've tracked down people with more money than Glory's Temple and meaner than the elves who run the EVP."

It was a naked threat, but something was altogether scarier about the way he leaned in close when he murmured, "You don't stand a chance, doll. Stop risking yourself. If you got hurt, I'd be an absolute pill to live with."

He knew she had no idea what she was doing. Instinct alone wouldn't help her. If he had experience hunting down people who had money and resources at their disposal, then how in the world was she supposed to escape him?

Damn. Carmine couldn't look at him. She turned sharply so that her feet rested in the footwell and stared out the windshield. Hopelessness, a familiar, dreadful feeling, wormed its way into her chest.

Atticus didn't push for a response. He must have known he won. Instead, he closed her door, picked up the bag, and wandered around to the driver's side. He sat with the bag in his lap for a second. After some rifling, he reached behind him to drop it with a heavy *thwump* onto the floor.

"Here."

Carmine blinked her stinging eyes when several small things tumbled into her lap. Her breath whooshed out of her in one massive gust.

It was Atticus's turn to avert his eyes as he started the vehicle. "I know you probably want better stuff, and you should pick things out yourself, but I figured — Well, I swiped some things I think Adriana— my sister likes. You don't have to use any of it, but..." He shrugged.

Like it was nothing.

She cradled the things he'd bought her in shaking hands: a

silky, cloth-covered hair tie, a tube of cherry flavored lip gloss, and a sparkly, pink-themed quad eyeshadow palette.

Her voice came out as barely more than a whisper when she said, "Will this be added to my debt?"

"Debt?"

"For your help. For everything." She traced the corner of the palette, her finger shaking. "At the crypt, the debt for our care went into our bride price. If we left, we or our family would have to pay it. Is this like that?"

Atticus's voice came out like crushed gravel when he answered, "No, Carmine. It's not like that. This is a gift."

"Really?"

"Fuckin' really, doll." He paused, then added, "There are no debts here. No tallying. No receipts piling up. You don't owe me shit, no matter what I do or what I spend on you. Got it?"

"Not really. I don't feel comfortable getting gifts."

"How about this?" He waited until she met his gaze before offering, "If you *want* to make things even, then how about every time I do something nice, you tell me a little something about you?"

Carmine gave him a look the proposal deserved. "How would that be an even trade?"

"It wouldn't be." He gave her a wink. "Trust me, I'm making out like a bandit on the deal."

She glanced back at her treasures. "Really?"

"Fuckin' really-really."

"I... Okay."

It was hard to see much with her eyes watering so bad, but it was impossible to miss the flash of his grin. She hadn't seen a lot of them, but she was certain Atticus had the best smile in the world.

"If you want something, you ask for it. Okay? I don't care if you think it's silly or a waste of money." He reached over to give her knee a small, playful nudge. "Let me put that look on your face some more, and let me hear that voice."

"What look?"

"The happy one."

Carmine's heart had lodged itself in her throat, so she couldn't reply to that even if she knew what to say. Instead, she ducked her head and, gathering her treasures close to her chest, decided, *Option B it is.*

Chapter Nine

Carmine spent most of the next two nights of their long drive contemplating how one went about being defiled. She knew the mechanics. They'd given brides all sorts of lessons about anatomy, reproduction, and sexual health. Spouses paid top dollar for their brides, so that meant they had to arrive fully educated and ready to do their duty.

She learned ways to pleasure a partner, no matter what anatomy they sported, and she understood the intricacies of reproduction. Carmine knew it might take a year or more to become pregnant, since her body needed to acclimate to her groom's venom first, and that both the process of becoming pregnant and giving birth would be deeply challenging.

She also knew the facts she'd faced on her slab: what a body looked like when it carried a child and when it hadn't and the various shapes and colors of sexual organs.

But seduction? Enticement? Carmine had no basis for that. It was always a given that she would be the one who endured advances, not the one giving them. She had no idea where to start.

It didn't help that Atticus was hugely intimidating. There wasn't a single moment when she wasn't aware of him. Every rustle of his clothing, every soft sound, every brush of his fingers

— he took up more space in her mind than he did in the RV, which was really saying something.

It didn't help that she was fairly certain he wasn't interested in her. That should have been a relief, but for some reason it rankled. *Fuck no,* he'd said.

Good. She didn't want to be anyone's blood bride.

But she needed him to defile her so *no one* would want her, and also... Well, it didn't feel nice to get that reaction.

Whatever. I can still do this.

Carmine only needed one chance, one moment, one person. If not him, then maybe he'd know someone who could do it. Surely there had to be a person out there willing to take her virginity who wouldn't expect to keep her, right?

It certainly sounded like there were a lot of people on Empire Estate. Atticus had filled her silences between unremarkable facts about her life with his low, raspy voice. He told her about how it used to be a gold mine, and that Harlan had a good crew of men he'd taken with him from the New Zone. They all lived on or around the estate and worked for him, either helping him with his many businesses or doing security, and not all of them were vampires, so she didn't have to worry about unwanted advances. Someone would always be around to keep her safe.

Would one of those men help her? It was a risk to wait that long. What if Atticus was lying? She was beginning to believe he wasn't, but she knew well that anyone could lie or change their mind. Carmine was entirely powerless. If it turned out he wasn't driving her to the fairytale land of stone cottages and witches named Zia and all the glittery eyeshadow she wanted, then what could she do?

Nothing. Nothing but ruin the one thing the crypt's matron told her was most important.

No one wants a bride who's been sullied. Be like the Merciful One. Be pure so your line will be untainted and your blood sweet.

Carmine's virginity was a weight around her neck. A target. A glaring neon sign that marked her as prey. She wanted to throw it out the RV's window and watch it burst into a thousand pieces. Maybe ask Atticus to reverse over it.

Her mind churned as she rolled a bottle of synth between her palms. Atticus kept trying to get her to drink, but she didn't like the taste of the brand he bought to replace what was in the RV already. The other was too chemically. This one was too bland.

He kept casting her dark looks that usually preceded a command for her to drink, but she ignored him. If he hadn't punished her for her escape attempts, she felt reasonably confident he wouldn't do it over a little synth.

"Who's Michael?"

Atticus didn't jump at her sudden question, but his rough, tattooed knuckles went white on the steering wheel. "Why?"

"You said he was going to pick me up. When you were talking to Harlan the other night."

"He's one of the boss's crew," he answered, scowling. "A demon. Nice enough, but he's not a talker."

Neither was she. Carmine could work with that.

She tilted her head, considering, flipping through the few demons she'd met on her slab. They were very interesting. They had horns or antlers, depending on the clan, and they were built so sturdy it took extra effort to prepare their bodies for burial. Her needles liked to bend when she pushed them through, fixing whatever was broken or torn or contorted in death, and she had to use pliers to get a good enough grip.

A demon could probably protect her. She'd read things about how devoted they were to mates. That could work.

Her goal was to lose her virginity and disappear, but there was always another option: She could find a good, strong mate. It didn't sit right with her, not when she knew they'd expect her to give up her work, but maybe things would be different if he wasn't a vampire — something she'd never even contemplated.

The bland synth went sour in her stomach at the thought of throwing herself at a man she'd never met, but she asked, "Does he have a mate?"

Atticus's head whipped around. His eyes went narrow and dangerous in a way she hadn't seen since that first night when he peered at her over the barrel of his gun. "Why the fuck are you asking?"

Carmine tried very hard not to tense. The fear that he'd discover her plan was a cold, hard weight in her gut. *He can't know. If he knows, he'll try and stop me.*

Forget about not being able to seduce him. If he suspected she was trying to lose her virginity by any means necessary, he wouldn't let her leave his sight. She'd never get the chance.

Lying was not her strong suit, but she'd learned that sometimes saying a part of the truth was good enough.

"I was curious," she hedged. "You made it sound like only Harlan has an anchor. Are all the other men single?" *Please say yes.*

Atticus looked like he'd just smelled something foul. Moving his attention back to the road, he bit out, "Yes."

Another thought occurred to her. A *zing* of something went down her spine. It wasn't pleasant. It was very much *not* like the times he smiled at her. "Do you have an anchor?" *Please say no.*

"No." And going by his tone, not to mention how he'd reacted to the idea of her being his bride, she guessed he didn't want one.

That was a good thing. It meant that if she *did* seduce him — by the gods, she still had to try, her ego be damned — he wouldn't try to keep her. She could be sullied and then on her way.

"Drink your synth," Atticus growled.

Carmine wasn't a fan of how it made her feel knowing he didn't want her. She could understand logically that it was good, but when she looked at him and felt that deep, dark pull in the pit of her stomach, she wanted something she had no name for — not to mention a hunger she couldn't satisfy with synth and an ache in her fangs that made her want to rip them out by the roots.

And that made her irritable. His bottle sat nearly untouched in the cupholder. What right did he have to order her to drink when he wouldn't?

"You drink *your* synth," she snapped back, pitifully churlish.

Atticus glowered at the road, lit by the beams of the RV's headlights. "I have plenty of mass to burn. You don't. Drink, Carmine."

Never in her life had she lacked an appetite. Except for immediately after a meal, she always felt the rumblings of hunger. Like most venom neutral vampires, she struggled to keep on weight. They had higher metabolisms than most vampires. She'd read that it had something to do with their predisposition toward consuming the blood of other vampires and their unusual venom production that messed with their nutritional needs, but the research on the subject was inadequate.

Whatever the reason, brides drank nearly twice as much synth as an average vampire. Their appetites were endless, which made it a perfect target for exploitation. The best punishment for a bride was simply cutting their meals down.

Atticus seemed to know she needed more synth than him. He was constantly hounding her to drink more. To finish his bottle. To go grab another and sip as he drove.

Unfortunately, for the first time in her life, Carmine didn't want synth. She wasn't sure if it was all the upheaval and stress or just that she was unlucky with the brands he'd chosen, but it tasted foul. She could barely force it down, no matter how empty her stomach felt.

Complaining wasn't going to get her anywhere. He paid for the synth, so what could she say? She knew that she ought to force it down and be grateful. But her venom gland wouldn't stop aching, her fangs hurt, fear about her future held her by the throat, and she was *hungry*.

She didn't think it through before she dropped her bottle into the cupholder beside his. Agitated, stifled by the air that tasted like him and the restless need that couldn't be named, she fumbled with her seatbelt until it unlatched. An alarm went off, presumably to alert her that she needed to put it back on, but she didn't care.

"What are you— Carmine, sit your ass *down.*" One big, tattooed paw reached for her, but she was already squirming out of his reach. The vehicle slowed, the sudden change in speed making her sway and clutch the wall as she tried to make her way to the back.

"Where are you going?" Atticus barked. "Carmine, you need to be strapped in. If we got into an accident—"

She wasn't sure why she was so mad at him or where her temper came from. Carmine wasn't a fighter. She was a thinker. A listener. A planner. And yet... "Are you a bad driver?"

It sounded like it came from between his teeth when he answered, "No."

"Then don't crash."

"Doll, if you don't sit your ass down, I'm gonna pull over."

She planned on curling up in the bed and stewing on how to rid herself of her virginity, but she wasn't about to tell him that, so she asked, "So? What'll you do then?"

There was a moment of taut silence. Her heart raced. For a second she thought it was dread that made her blood rush, but that wasn't right. She knew the anticipation that came just before a punishment. The fear. The swooping feeling of helplessness.

This wasn't the same.

She kept walking, determined to keep her footing as the RV jostled over the road, but she was keenly aware of the vampire at her back. He *could* do anything to her. Atticus hadn't punished her yet, but that didn't mean he wouldn't. A couple of trinkets from a gas station didn't mean he was a good guy.

So why wasn't she afraid?

Just as she reached the bed, Atticus breathed deep and said, "You're upset."

Well, she had nothing to say to that, did she? So she didn't reply. Carmine pulled the covers back with some force, yanking the blankets out of the tight corners she folded every dusk, and slid rebelliously beneath the covers.

She couldn't remember the last time she'd simply gone back to bed. It never would have been allowed at the crypt. There was always some lesson to be learned, some work to be done. Taking a nap would have been seen as slovenly behavior.

Maybe that was why she was pitching a fit. She'd never sat so long in one place in her life. She didn't have her work to occupy her. Just her thoughts, her worries, and *him*.

Fuck no, he'd said.

Drink your synth, he'd ordered.

Well, if he wasn't going to be her groom, then he could shove his orders somewhere tender.

Jerk.

"Carmine—"

"I'm sitting down like you wanted," she told him, using a tone she never would have gotten away with in the crypt. Adrenaline raced through her veins as she turned on her side to face the wall.

She blinked. All at once, her ire deflated like a popped corpse. *Why am I challenging him? I've got nothing to be mad about. Not really.*

Carmine understood that she was stressed and physically uncomfortable, but that had never made her so reckless or irritable before. It'd simply never been safe enough for her to risk it.

Oh. That embarrassed, crawly feeling washed over her.

She wished she'd had the forethought to change into the shirt he let her borrow. The matron had included two plain night dresses in her box of clothing, but she'd conveniently left them in the trailer. Atticus's shirt was more comfortable and it smelled better, like something spicy and rich that made her mouth water.

"Dollface, if you talk to me, I can make whatever it is you're upset about better." There was a pause, then, quieter, "I'd *like* to make it better."

Her stomach cramped with hunger, and she was forced to swallow a mouthful of saliva as a wave of need hit her. It wasn't just the need to eat, but an impulse that made the muscles of her jaw flex. It was the instinct to *bite*.

The madness that had possessed her to throw a fit was gone and replaced by another sort: the urge to be near the person who made her feel *safe*.

It was on the tip of her tongue to tell him. Carmine desperately wanted to believe that everything he said was true, that she could trust him to help her, but what if she was wrong? The risks terrified her. If she told him that she needed him to take her virginity, he'd see all her cards. The only bit of power over her own life she had left would vanish in an instant.

So she didn't tell him. Instead, she reached beneath her pillow and retrieved her treasures. After sliding the scrunchy onto her wrist, she occupied herself with reading the instructions on the back of the eyeshadow palette and the ingredient list on the lip gloss tube.

She read it and she thought, *How hard can seduction be, anyway?*

CHAPTER TEN

NEITHER OF THEM HAD EATEN MUCH. ATTICUS KNEW Carmine needed to eat more than him, so she had to be starving. That pissed him off, especially when it was because she just wanted to be stubborn.

But that wasn't the only reason for his temper. She wasn't the sole source of his problems. *He* hadn't eaten, either, and that was very, very bad.

Atticus was strung tight as a bow. Even the fine muscles in his fingers were tense as he lowered the shades on the windows. He was hyper-aware of Carmine. She hadn't spoken a word since she stormed off halfway through the night, but that only made him *more* focused on her.

It didn't matter that the engine rumbled or the heating unit buzzed on the roof. He could still hear every single one of her breaths, every slight shift on the bed. His mouth watered at the taste of cherry in the air. As he drove, every one of his instincts screamed at him to pull over and do what biology demanded: feed and breed.

The need was so strong, he hadn't been able to choke synth down. It tasted like ash compared to the sweet earthiness he knew was only a few feet away, tucked beneath thin sheets.

It was deeply, profoundly wrong for him to want her as bad as he did. Biology was fucking with him and so were the gods, probably. It was a great cosmic joke to lock him in a vehicle with someone so unattainable.

He couldn't lay a hand on her, let alone a fang. He was the lowest sort of scum to be thinking of how good Carmine would taste, or how fucking beautiful those eyes would look when he thrust his cock inside her.

Atticus wanted to think he had good willpower. He'd been raised by Harlan Bounds. The man was all steel, and he'd taught Atticus to be the same way. Of course, with family things were different, but to *protect* their family, they needed to be harder than their enemies.

He didn't give in to impulse. He wasn't someone who was *tempted*. He didn't fuck around, and he didn't take risks.

But he couldn't swallow another mouthful of synth, and he was beginning to worry that it wasn't the flavor that was the issue. He'd bought his favorite brand. There was no reason for it to taste so bad, even allowing for slight differences in batches.

Atticus had heard stories of how vampires could instinctively reject any blood that didn't come from the potential anchor they'd fixed on, but if he thought too hard about that, he thought he might hand Carmine his gun and tell her to aim for his head.

She seemed soft and sweet, but he was pretty sure she'd do it.

It was deeply worrying how even that thought made him hard.

Stop thinking with your cock and figure out what's wrong.

Left to stew in silence for hours, he couldn't shake the vague memory of something Harlan said after he and Zia got together. *"Once I saw her, synth never tasted the same."*

They were no Harlan and Zia, who'd been obsessed with each other since the moment they crossed paths. Those two were soulmates. He and Carmine were just... stuck together. That was all it was.

Atticus wanted to fix whatever had upset her, but the idea of getting near her scared the shit out of him. He adjusted the shade again, making sure it completely covered the window, and tried not to dwell on the fact that he was now both a creep and a coward.

Turning toward the bed, he was tempted to ask her if she wanted to go for a walk. They could both use the fresh air, and sunrise wasn't for a while yet. But then he remembered how she'd bolted last time, and the way she'd nearly smashed her face in when she tried to escape from the window. They'd been getting along, building trust, but after their fight, he didn't want to take any risks. Until he could trust she wouldn't do something reckless, they were both stuck in the RV.

Running a trembling hand through his hair, Atticus forced himself to walk at a normal pace. His legs wanted to run to her, but his brain balked at crossing the short distance.

He needed to get a grip. How could he help her if his head was a disaster? Atticus knew better than this. He'd been *raised* to be better than this.

Atticus gritted his teeth and slowly sank onto the edge of the mattress. Carmine was huddled against the wall, hidden beneath the sheets, but he could tell by how tense she was that she wasn't asleep.

"Doll," he rasped, daring to give her ankle a featherlight squeeze. "C'mon. You've been ignoring me all night. If you won't tell me what's wrong, then can I at least see your pretty eyes?"

"Why?"

"Because I'm worried about—"

"Why do you think they're pretty?"

Oh. Atticus blinked. Most women would have taken his compliment at face value or dismissed it altogether, but of course Carmine didn't. He got the sense that she took nothing at face value. Everything was mulled over, picked apart, and reassembled in that keen brain of hers.

Normally he wouldn't have minded explaining himself to her. Unfortunately, that particular question made heat crawl up the back of his neck. "You, uh... They're blue. And big. You've got nice eyelashes, too."

They're fucking gorgeous, and when they look at me, I can't feel the ground under my feet anymore. Because I'm a rabid, horny idiot who should be put down with a tranq gun or a brick at your earliest convenience.

"Do you think *I'm* pretty?"

Atticus began to sweat. Too late he realized he'd never taken his hand off her ankle. It'd turned into a shackle. No matter how hard he tried, he couldn't pry his fingers loose.

"Yes," he answered, so hoarse it barely sounded like a word.

Carmine was silent for a second, leaving him in wordless agony, before she asked, "Would someone else think I was pretty? Michael?"

He'd had broken bones before. Plenty of them. He'd also broken more than his fair share in other people.

Carmine's innocent question shouldn't have meant anything to him, but when the words hit him, he felt a familiar wet snap somewhere in his chest. Like she'd reached into him with one of those perfect, delicate hands and broken a rib as easily as snapping a twig.

Blood roared in his ears. For a split second, he could have sworn his vision went black. Then it went red.

It was a very, very good thing that Michael was still a thousand miles away. If he'd been there, Atticus wouldn't have hesitated. There would have been no thoughts, no regrets. The instinct to fight for an anchor, to annihilate all competition, was so loud it drowned out every civilized notion he might have once possessed.

But Michael wasn't there. He was back on the estate, innocently going about his business, maybe chasing after Serafina to give her parents a break or shooting the shit with the other guards. The knowledge that he had no idea what Carmine even looked like, let alone spoken to her, helped dull the sharpest edge of Atticus's rage. Enough to speak, at least.

"What the fuck is with you and Michael?" The urge to rip the sheets away from her so he could see her face was a loud, mean one, but he still had some sense in his head. He was jealous, not completely heartless. If he started losing his cool like that, she'd freak out and never trust him. Rightfully so.

Luckily he didn't have to wrestle with the urge for too long before Carmine's huge blue eyes peeked at him from beneath the sheets. Little red claws, filed down and glossy, gripped the edge by her cheek.

"I was just wondering."

"Yeah? Well, stop wondering. Of course he'll think you're pretty. Everyone will. You're gorgeous, Carmine. Anyone who looks at you is fuckin' blessed. Got it? But if I hear a word about Michael anywhere near you, I'll—"

Atticus somehow managed to stop himself before he said something he had no right to say. Carmine could seek out whatever companionship she desired. Michael could, too. What if it turned out that she was the demon's mate?

Demons would tear down the whole world for their mates, and that was exactly what Carmine needed. Someone who'd go to war if she was threatened. Someone who'd risk everything to keep her safe. Someone who'd let her explore who she wanted to be and who'd give her all the glittery shit her heart desired and welcome her perfect little bite and—

But when Atticus tried to picture it, when he imagined Carmine gracefully crossing the threshold of Michael's cottage with a lovesick smile on her face, her arm wrapped in the demon's symbiotic shadows and her skin covered in his scent...

Atticus's world went red again.

Chapter Eleven

A SOFT HAND TOUCHED HIS THIGH. THE MUSCLE jumped. His eyes swung back to Carmine, his vision tunneling until she was his sole focus. She'd dropped the sheets and sat up. Her hair was mussed and her cheeks were flushed.

He didn't like how cautious she sounded when she asked, "Why are you mad? What did I do? I'm sorry about earlier. I don't know why I threw a fit. I've never— I'm sorry."

"You didn't do anything," he snapped, forcing his hands into fists by his sides. He tried to clear the rage out of his mind, to really think of why she might ask the questions she had. When he came up with an answer, the rush of shame was immediate. "If you're thinking of shacking up with someone because you're worried about your future, don't. You don't need to. We're going to help you get on your feet, Carmine. You don't have to— You're going to be safe. I promise."

Forcing a smile, he added, "And for the record, I take it as a compliment that you got pissy with me. That means you feel comfortable. We're good, I swear."

"Okay." She didn't sound like she believed him, but how could he blame her?

Atticus swiped a hand down his face. He was flushed, sweaty.

Aggression still bunched his muscles. He would have done anything to go for a run in the cool night air.

But even if he could trust Carmine not to escape, the idea of leaving her exposed made his skin crawl. He needed her back home. Somewhere dark and safe. Somewhere like his bedroom, which was once a root cellar but had been converted to a luxurious suite. It didn't have windows and it remained cool even on the hottest days of the year.

A deep, primal urge demanded he lock her inside and never let her leave.

Switching to rub the back of his neck, Atticus dared to look at her. She was watching him warily, like she knew exactly what he was thinking. Maybe she did. He wasn't the first vampire to crave her. Junger probably had dreams of locking her up, too.

Fucker.

At least he'd never act on it, and Junger would be dead soon, anyway. The thought of how satisfying it would be to see the light leave his eyes was enough to calm Atticus down.

His head wasn't screwed on right, but at least he had some sense back. Enough to notice how bad Carmine looked. Eyeing her dark circles and gaunt cheeks, an alarm sounded in the forefront of his mind.

She's starving.

If his aversion to synth hadn't told him enough, the screeching worry he experienced over her hunger was undeniable. It didn't matter that he knew she wasn't his. Instinct was instinct. When a vampire fixed on a potential anchor, they became single-minded about their care and keeping.

Yeah, he would have cared about anyone going hungry, but this was different. If an anchor starved, so did a vampire. The urge to provide for them was a hardwired survival imperative.

He was up and lurching across the short distance to the kitchenette before he'd made the choice to do so, and certainly before he could process the staggering confirmation of what instinct and desire were trying to tell him. "You need to eat," he barked. "How many bottles have you had since you left the crypt?"

He didn't give her the chance to answer. Tearing a bottle from the pack, he gave it a shake and then twisted the lid. The seal cracked and the bottle began to heat in his hand.

"Here." He sat back down on the bed and shoved it under her nose. "Drink. I'm not moving until you do."

Carmine curled her shoulders and turned her head away, her nose wrinkled like she'd smelled something foul. He expected her to refuse, but she didn't say anything at all.

"Carmine," he pressed, voice tight with worry. "Doll, you *have* to drink. You're killing me. Please just take a sip."

She squished her face into her raised knees and mumbled something. His brow wrinkled. "What was that?"

"I can't drink that."

He glanced at the bottle. "Why?"

She went quiet again. Reluctantly lowering his arm, he used his free hand to brush her dark hair out of her eyes. She peeked at him from under the fringe of her lashes. "Why, doll?"

There was a moment of hesitation. "I hate the taste. Really hate it. I can't get it down."

Atticus stopped breathing. "You..." He cleared his throat. Tried again. "You don't like the taste? What about the other kind?" There were still plenty of bottles of the brand Junger's lackeys stocked. She had options.

Carmine shook her head.

"Is there— Is there a brand that sounds good? A flavor you want?" He shifted his feet and flexed his fingers around the bottle. "Are you doing a hunger strike, doll?"

She shook her head again.

Holy fuck. Sweat dewed on the back of his neck. He knew how Adriana's appetite was. If Carmine was similar, the fact that she couldn't just force herself to drink the synth was...

Good gods, she wants me.

Did she even know what her aversion to synth meant? He

doubted it. Why would they teach her that in the crypt? He knew blood brides were sometimes taught that they would be fed on, but not that it would be reciprocated. *That* was supposed to be the purest form of matehood, the perfect vampiric circle, but most of the shitheads who bought brides didn't like the idea of being fed on. It was some macho man bullshit.

Atticus was not an idiot, nor did he subscribe to any macho man bullshit. Even though it felt taboo in the extreme, he was honored to have her see him as a potential anchor, even if she didn't know that herself.

Honored and catastrophically turned on.

His throat worked hard to swallow the saliva that pooled in his mouth as he tried to find a solution to their issue. Carmine needed to eat — desperately. She couldn't miss another meal. If she did, he worried he'd be forced to take her to a clinic for an IV, and that would turn shit tits up in an instant.

But if she couldn't drink synth, then...

His breath went short. His cock was pinched behind his zipper. Competing impulses warred in his mind. One wanted to offer her his throat and the other wanted to sink his fangs into hers.

He was a jumble of needs, all of them blaring sirens in his head, but in the end, it was the innate protectiveness of his anchor that won out.

And maybe a bit of selfishness and curiosity, too.

Atticus's joints felt wooden as he slowly turned to set the bottle on the floor. His palms were sweaty. He pressed them flat against his thighs. *You can do this. Be cool. Be normal. Don't wig her out.*

"C'mere." It came out so much rougher than he intended, but it was a miracle he spoke actual words at all.

Carmine blinked at him. "What?"

"Come here," he said again, clearer this time. Keeping steady eye contact with her, he explained, "If you can't drink synth, then you're gonna drink something, doll."

It was a thing of beauty, watching her pupils blow up like that. One minute her eyes were dark blue and the next they were black. Her lips parted. A flush infused the tops of her high cheekbones. Her blunt little claws curled into the blankets. "You— you don't mean I should—"

"I sure do." He tugged at the blankets, pulling them out of her grip. When her legs were exposed, he patted his thigh. "It doesn't have to mean anything. You take what you need."

Even as he said it, he knew that was absurd. Of course it would mean something. It meant something for a vampire to bite anyone. It was *sacred* for a vampire to bite another.

She'd be injecting her venom into his blood. Sure, it took regular injections to make the bond take, but for just a second he'd belong to her and her alone. He'd sustain her. If he bit her back, she'd have his venom, too. A perfect circle of protection and intimacy.

It would never mean *nothing*. Even if it was just the once.

It would always mean *everything*.

A part of him had braced for her argument, but Carmine only stared at him for what felt like an eternity before she slowly got onto her hands and knees. His pulse jumped at the sight of her crawling toward him. And when he noticed her watching his throat, where blood throbbed just beneath his skin, he had to bite his lip to keep from reaching for his cock. He had no idea what he planned to do with it, since he absolutely could not put it anywhere near her, but if he didn't get some relief soon, he was pretty sure he'd lose his mind.

Atticus turned his body to face her, one boot on the floor and his other leg bent on the bed. Before he could talk himself out of it, he settled his hands on her waist and guided her to straddle him. He swallowed a groan when she bunched her long dress around her hips and settled herself down on his thigh. His hands itched to wander, but he sat rigidly beneath her, grasping at control that slipped from him like smoke.

"Are you *sure?*" He wasn't the only one with a husky voice, apparently. Carmine's high tones were tempered with something rich and smoky when she tentatively rested her hands on his shoulders.

"Pretty fuckin' sure," he muttered. Unsticking his hand from her waist with some difficulty, he hooked a finger under his collar and pulled. "Drink, doll."

He squeezed his eyes shut. Not because he didn't want to look, but because he worried about what he'd do if he watched her. This wasn't supposed to be a sexual thing. It was a simple, biological need. He refused to be the creep who took advantage of a vulnerable woman.

The softest fingertips brushed his throat, tracing tendons and the contours of his flesh. "You're so warm." It was a whisper. He wasn't even sure she was talking to him.

"You are, too," he replied, like an idiot. She was burning up in his lap, particularly where her cunt kissed the seam of his pants. She practically *blazed* there. Didn't mean he had to say it, though.

"I like your tattoos." Her hot breath kissed his throat. The fingers that explored him settled on the bar of his collar bone, trembling. "I don't want to ruin them."

"They'll be fine. Bites heal clean." And he wouldn't care if they didn't. He'd let her ruin any part of him she liked. He wanted her to.

Fuck me, I might even beg for it.

She didn't reply. Soft lips brushed his skin, sending a searing wave of sensation down his spine. He felt that tiny touch all the way to his damn *toes*. Something like a kiss — so tentative, so very sweet it almost didn't count — nearly knocked him on his ass.

And that was before the bite.

All vampires had the instinct, but it took some practice to get good at it, to not go too fast, too deep, or too shallow. Something dark and possessive in him purred with satisfaction when Carmine went shallow. He had to gently press on the back of her head to encourage her to go deeper.

*There's no way she's done this with someone else. Just me.
Only me.*

It was both perverse and yet sacred to be on the other end of
the bite, but the moment her precious little fangs slid through his
flesh, all sting and then glowy warmth, Atticus knew he was a
goner. There was no going back from this.

The pleasure was instant. As soon as her venom hit his blood-
stream, he let out a long, low groan and wrapped his arm around
her back to clutch her opposite shoulder, clasping her to him like
he feared she'd stop.

He knew that in a few seconds, her venom would stop flow-
ing. She'd extract her fangs. She'd use her perfect tongue to make a
little suction and drink from him. He knew the mechanics
because he'd done it many times to different partners, but he
never knew it felt like *this.*

Carmine didn't make a sound, but her hands wandered,
petting, soothing, driving him wild as she extracted her fangs. Her
tongue was hot and wet, her lips smooth. When she began to pull
from him, he let out a low, reflexive shout.

She startled and tried to pull back, but he quickly cupped the
back of her head again. Holding here there. *Can't let her go.
Won't.*

"No," he gasped, "keep going. Please. Take more, doll. Take
what you need."

It took her a second, but she got back into the flow. She
melted until she was wrapped around him, clinging to him, their
bodies pressed together as intimately as they could be while still
clothed.

He was desperate to rock his hips. All he needed was the
slightest bit of friction and he'd go off like a teenager. Gods help
him if one of those hands snuck down to pop the button on his
pants. He'd be done in seconds.

Don't. You can't. She didn't ask for any of that.

But that didn't stop him from turning his nose into her hair
to breathe her in. It didn't stop him from running his hand down

her back, feeling the elegant shape of her ribs and waist. It didn't stop him from—

He let out a low sound of complaint when she began to lap at him, closing the wound with her saliva. Atticus's breath sawed in and out of him. *We can't be done already. No, no, no.*

He wanted to demand she come back. He needed her to take more. If she moved away now, he'd lose every last shred of composure and beg her to stay.

His hands turned into vices on her waist as she sat back a little. Not away, but enough that they could look at each other. The change also resettled her weight — putting her right on top of his cock.

Atticus hissed and nearly lifted her by the hips, desperate to throw her off before he lost control of himself and did something unforgivable, but she rocked a little, just enough, and his good intentions burst like a bubble.

"Atticus?" Her voice was so soft, so blissed out, and the clumsy, shy rocking motions of her hips were so needy.

He gave in to the desire to look at her. *Fuck.*

She was staring at him with huge, blissed out eyes. Her lips were a little swollen and stained. They parted, so he could see the blood that painted her perfect pink tongue, too. It was on her breath, running down her throat, sustaining her.

He made a sound he'd never made before: some strange cross between a whine and a growl. The roots of his fangs throbbed in his gums. He wanted to *devour* her.

Like she'd read his mind, Carmine reached for his hand and guided it down. "Please touch me."

"I shouldn't." So why was his hand sliding under the bunched fabric of her dress? Because he was a bad person, probably. Definitely. No one was good enough to touch Carmine, but he had to be lowest on the list by far.

Carmine cupped his jaw and looked at him like— He had no idea. It was some mix of awe and academic interest, like she was trying to savor the moment but also like he was a wet specimen in a jar, soon to be dissected so her keen mind could understand how he worked. It was hot as fuck.

"I want you to," she whispered, leaning forward to brush her lips against his cheek experimentally. "Please, Atticus. Touch me."

He was ruined.

"Fuck. *Fuck.*" He didn't stand a chance. As soon as his fingers hit the soaked gusset of her panties, he was done for. "Did drinking from me make you this wet, doll?"

She paused like she had to think about it. Maybe she did. "Yes."

"Did you like how I tasted?"

That got a much more immediate response. "Yes. Very much. I want more."

That answer deserved a reward. Atticus slid his fingers inside her panties and found hot, silky flesh. *Gods have mercy on me.* A single exploratory touch soaked his fingers. She was *dripping* for him. From one taste.

Slick flesh, smooth as silk and hot as fire, scalded his fingers. She was gorgeous everywhere, and when her desire perfumed the air, it was a high the likes of which he'd never experienced.

"Doll," he breathed, rubbing slow, gentle circles and watching her cheeks flush, "do you want me to make you come?"

"More than I've ever wanted anything, I think." She answered in that peculiar, frank way of hers and it had absolutely no right being as sexy as it was. He loved that. There was something so genuine about her, so honest and confident. Carmine didn't hedge her answers or dance around self-consciously. She was just as likely to say something he wouldn't like as she was to tell him yes, she *did* want him to make her see stars.

Atticus had never been so turned on in his life, and he'd certainly never *grinned* as he played with a woman's cunt before, but there he was. He was scum, but fuck it, he was the happiest scum on Burden's Earth.

"You tell me to stop if you're uncomfortable. The second you hesitate, this ends. No questions. No hard feelings. Got it?"

Carmine nodded impatiently.

"Confirmation, doll," he pressed, stilling his hand.

Her hips bucked. Panting, she muttered, "Confirmation. Stop. Uncomfortable. Got it. Yes. *Please* move your fingers."

And because he was apparently an asshole as well as scum, he asked, "Why? You like my fingers on your perfect pussy, doll?"

"Yes," she answered immediately, devastating any shreds of his willpower that remained. "I like your fingers. I like your mouth. Your face. I love your tattoos and your voice and when I smell you, my fangs *ache.*"

He lost his head. That was why he snapped. Kissing her was the only sensible thing to do at that moment. Cupping the back of her neck with his free hand, Atticus crushed their mouths together.

Carmine yelped, but she didn't pull away. Her fingers slid into his hair and held fast as he tasted his blood on her tongue, tasted *her.* She was clumsy, a little shy, but the longer he stroked her cunt, the more her confidence grew. Her hips rocked and her nails curled into his scalp. Soon enough she was angling her head for more.

She started making noise. That was a surprise. Carmine was so quiet normally that he didn't expect her to gasp and moan and make soft little kitten sounds when he slid a finger inside her and stroked her g-spot while the heel of his palm ground down on her clitoris.

Atticus had tasted the best alcoholic synth in the world. He knew what it was to be intoxicated. Watching Carmine ride his hand as she licked his blood from her lips was better, headier, than that.

When she broke their kiss to toss her head back and *scream,* her arms banded around him so tightly that her shoulders shook, Atticus met the gods for the first time in his life.

Half-feral and not anywhere close to done with her, he wrapped the fingers of his free hand around her throat and extracted his other hand from her panties. Her scent, cherry and musk and sweet cunt, exploded in his mouth when he sucked his fingers clean.

Carmine sat in his lap, limp and heavy-lidded, her arms draped over his shoulders. Her thighs shook around his hips. She looked like she had been kissed to within an inch of her life. He loved that look on her. He wanted to see it fixed there permanently.

And then she reached for the button of his pants and in her pretty, sated voice asked, "Are you going to defile me now?"

CHAPTER TWELVE

Atticus was mad at her. Really mad.

He wouldn't talk to her. She didn't think she'd miss it, seeing as she was used to silence, but at some point she'd acclimated to his chatter.

Carmine sat in the passenger's seat, her hands flat on her knees, and stared out at the road. They'd passed out of the desert and had begun to wind through mountains. They took strange, twisty roads where they almost never passed another vehicle. She wasn't sure why, but she guessed it had something to do with avoiding cities or authorities.

They never said it in the crypt, but it didn't take a genius to understand that something about her situation was illegal. The authorities wouldn't have shown up at their door otherwise, and the priests wouldn't have scrambled to sell their brides so quickly if they didn't worry about what would happen if they were caught.

I wonder if they gave a discount on me.

She didn't want to be a blood bride, so what did she care that she was the last to go? They always said she was too tall. That she should have tried harder at her music lessons, her budgeting classes, her childcare scores. Everything that might have made her a more desirable bride had either been out of her reach due to lack of natural skill or simply uninteresting to her.

It wasn't that the other brides flew out the door regularly. No one wanted a bride that was too young, since the likelihood of conception increased dramatically after thirty. Like her, most of the brides were there for decades, often from the time before they could properly talk. They had to fill their time with something, and the matron encouraged pursuits that would make them more desirable.

The thought that she was perhaps the least desirable of the lot had always cheered her up. Not now.

Now, sitting in tense silence after experiencing the best night of her life, she couldn't help but think of all those deficiencies, the parts of her that might make a man like Atticus choose someone more suitable.

Carmine dared to sneak a look at him. He sat like a statue in the driver's seat, his jaw clenched and his eyes unreadable. He hadn't spoken to her since she fed from him. No pushing bottles of synth her way. No explaining the route they were on.

No offers to let her drink again.

Her eyes inevitably drifted to the puncture wounds on his neck and the bloom of bruises around it. Her heart rate skyrocketed every time she saw it.

Carmine had never dreamed of feeding from another person before. She'd lived on synth all her life, and then the matron had always drilled it into their heads that their spouses would probably not allow them to bite. The few times she'd pictured it, the act had been purely mechanical — like poking a straw into a drink, or putting one's head under the tap rather than getting a glass. Nothing extraordinary. Just different than how she normally did it.

She couldn't have been more wrong.

Drinking from Atticus was *everything*. Not just because she felt completely full for the first time in her life, and not because it fulfilled an innate urge she'd never acknowledged.

It was him. The way he smelled. The warmth of his skin. The weight of his hands on her waist. The low, raspy rumble of his voice. When the bliss of releasing her venom hit her, some stranger took over her body, flushing her with needs she'd never even known existed.

Arousal. The craving not just for blood, but for touch. For his gruff noises, his hot, puffing breaths, the spotlight of his absolute focus on her and her alone.

She knew all about arousal because she'd read about it, had been instructed on how to stoke it in a partner. She knew that sexual interest came with a series of symptoms like lubrication, elevated heart rate, restlessness, and a higher body temperature. An orgasm was the end goal, and resulted in a rush of endorphins as well as biological material. If she was lucky, the matron explained, sex would be quick, fruitful, and relatively painless.

Why didn't anyone say it was like that?

Carmine wanted to storm back to the crypt and shake the old woman by the hair. If she'd known that it could feel like that, she would have tried to defile herself a decade ago.

The memory of his taste, the sounds he made, how he'd made her feel with his big, rough hands and hungry kisses haunted her every second of the night. As did the stupid word that had ruined it all: *defilement.*

Her orgasm and the lush meal she'd sipped from Atticus's throat were tainted by that word. As soon as it left her mouth, he'd gone cold and stiff, his expression almost horrified. In a choked voice, he'd asked, *"Is that what you're angling for, Carmine? Is that— Did you* plan *this?"*

She was too overwhelmed to try lying, so she'd remained silent, hoping he'd let it go and not notice the guilt written across her face. Of course it only took him a second to put it all together, and when he did...

Well, she supposed he could have reacted in worse ways than giving her the cold shoulder. It hurt, though.

It probably wouldn't have been so bad if he hadn't given her a taste of paradise before ripping it all away from her, but she had no one to blame for that but herself.

Drawing her knees up to her chest, she leaned away from him and turned her attention to the passenger's window. If he could be believed, this was the last night they'd be in the RV together. They'd meet whoever Harlan sent and she'd be passed off at dawn.

After that, there was no telling what would happen to her.

The thought terrified her. She didn't want to leave Atticus. Even when he was angry, he was at least familiar. His presence comforted her. He made her feel safe for the first time in her life. The thought of separating from him made her want to throw up the precious gift he'd given her.

Would Michael be nice? Or would she be passed off and find herself in a worse situation? What if she never saw Atticus again?

Something clawed at her insides when she imagined getting into a car without him. Something ugly and fearful. Something that *screamed*.

Atticus's anger had sucked all the air out of the RV, and that thing in her couldn't stand it. She understood seducing him came with risks, but Carmine underestimated how it would feel to be rejected, let alone endure his quiet sort of wrath.

Fuck no, he'd said. Why hadn't she taken the hint?

Her stomach turned again. Would she be able to try again with another man? A day ago she wouldn't have hesitated, but now she imagined it'd be a bit like answering the question, *"If you were trapped under a boulder, would you cut your arm off with a spoon to survive?"*

Yes, if her only other option was a slow death. But she didn't *want* to.

Carmine turned her face into her arms. Her hair slid over to create a curtain between them. She missed her veil. She missed being able to hide — not just her face, but everything about her. He'd seen her unveiled, inside and out. Her veil wouldn't have erased the fact that he knew more about her than anyone in the world, nor wipe away the memory of his touch, but it would have been a comfort, at least.

"Carmine."

She jumped. Her muscles coiled tight. He sounded gruff. Cold. Her heart fluttered wildly in her chest. Adrenaline made her head swim and her palms sweat. *Is this it?*

Any minute now he'd tell her that he'd lied, that something awful was coming and she was powerless to stop it. He'd tell her how repulsed he was by her attempt to seduce him and that she'd be lucky if he didn't tell her groom.

Unconsciously holding her breath, she gripped her arms so hard, her claws bit into her skin.

"We're coming up on an EVP checkpoint. I've already got pre-approval with the guard — he's a friend — but if we get stopped, just act normal and don't say anything."

She had no idea what normal meant. If he wasn't so angry at her, she would have asked him. Instead, she nodded and squeezed her eyes shut. *You're okay. It's just a checkpoint. He's not getting rid of you.*

Yet.

The checkpoint turned out to be little more than a small building with a gate attached to it that was lowered over the road. It blazed with light. Carmine squinted at it from over her arms, but otherwise didn't move. She barely breathed when Atticus pulled to a slow stop in front of the gate.

A moment later, a man with dark skin and a wide, gleaming smile strode out a door. He was adjusting something that looked a little bit like a cowboy hat on his head as he made his way to the driver's side window. Dressed in a crisp gray uniform and shiny badge, he looked perfectly at ease when he knocked on the window with a knuckle.

"That you, Caldwell?"

Nodding, Atticus replied, "Hey, John. You get my message?"

"Yup."

"Everything good?"

"Business as usual, 'cept we've got a supervisor in town," he replied, rolling his eyes. "Gotta make sure we earn those Sovereign-given benefits, I guess."

"Is that gonna be an issue for us?"

"Nah. You're a citizen. You can cross over." Carmine couldn't see much, but when she caught a glimpse of the brim of his hat, she thought he might be peering around Atticus to peek at her. "Who's that with you?"

Atticus shook his head. His tone changed, but Carmine had no idea what it meant. "A friend."

There was a pause. She desperately wished she could have seen Atticus's expression when John drawled, "Ah, I see how it is. Well—"

"Garcia."

Carmine looked up to find a tall figure standing in the doorway of the building. It took her a second to figure out what she was looking at, mostly because she'd never seen a being like them in person before.

Their skin was forest green, their ears pointed, and their hair shorn close to the scalp. The collar of their uniform was higher than John's. Or maybe it was just buttoned all the way up. Either way, it covered their entire throat. When they began to stride over, Carmine was amazed by the liquid grace they moved with.

That's an elf.

She knew they were headed to elvish territory, but for some reason she never considered that she'd see one of them.

John cleared his throat and stepped back from Atticus's window. "Captain," he muttered. "I was just giving these folks the all clear. The driver's a citizen."

"I see." The elf stopped by the front wheel. Carmine sat up a little so she could watch them through the windshield. Quick, dark eyes assessed the RV before locking onto Atticus. A brow arched. "Camping?"

"A road trip to pick up a friend," he answered, smooth as could be. "She's moving."

The elf's eyes didn't waver from Atticus. "What's in the trailer?"

"Just some boxes with her stuff."

"I scanned your RV. Is there a reason your vehicle is registered to the Neutral Zone if you're from the EVP?"

"I flew over there to pick her up," he answered with a casual flick of his fingers. "Seemed easier to rent an RV and trailer when I got there than lug them across the continent."

"Mind if I look inside the trailer?"

"Be my guest. You're gonna think I'm an idiot, though. I over-estimated how much shit she'd have, so it's mostly empty." A wry note entered his voice. If she didn't know the truth, Carmine would have believed him without hesitation. "She just left temple life, so I guess I should have known, but I've got a sister, so..." He shrugged.

The elf's expression didn't get any friendlier. They gestured for Atticus to get out of the vehicle.

Something in Carmine's chest went unbearably tight as she watched him unbuckle his seatbelt and open the door.

She must have made some kind of noise, because Atticus's head swiveled around to look at her. "Hey," he murmured, "it's okay. I'm not going anywhere, okay? This is routine stuff."

Carmine had no way of knowing if that was true or not, and she hated seeing him hop out of the RV. She hated watching him disappear, the elf and a tense John trotting behind him.

There was some noise, the sound of voices, and then they reappeared. It couldn't have taken longer than two minutes, but it felt like an eternity. She watched Atticus's face like a hawk as he climbed back inside. He looked totally unbothered.

Leaning an elbow out the open window, he asked, "We good to go?"

"One more thing."

The elf appeared again, but they didn't stop walking when they hit Atticus's window. This time, their eyes were trained on Carmine. "Miss, could you step out of the vehicle, please?"

Carmine's gaze flickered to Atticus. If she couldn't see the white-knuckled fist on the seat, hidden from the Patrol officers, she would have thought he was completely unconcerned. "She's shy," he said, tilting his head toward her. "Temple girl, remember? Might be best to just talk through the window."

The elf offered him a cold, close-lipped smile. "I'll be nice. Miss, if you could step out. I only want to ask a couple questions."

Carmine swallowed and glanced at Atticus again. He met her gaze. Something dark and inscrutable snaked through his eyes, but he nodded. "Everything's okay, doll. Don't worry. I'm right here."

Her hand trembled when she unlatched her belt and reached for the door. She wasn't even sure why, only that she perceived some danger in this situation. Not for her, but for Atticus.

She'd barely touched her slippers to the road before the elf gestured for her to step a bit away from the RV. Carmine felt all eyes on her as she shuffled over. Knotting her fingers in front of her, she waited for the elf to ask their questions.

"What's your name?" The elf's voice was almost unrecognizable. It was softer, lower. Gentle, almost. Carmine looked up in surprise and found the elf had their back to the RV. The headlights cast them in a soft yellow glow that scattered into a hundred different colors when it touched their skin and shorn hair. The cold captain was gone, replaced by someone with bright eyes and a deep frown.

"Carmine."

"Pretty. You got an ID, Carmine?"

"I... Yes, a chip." *I think.*

"Good. Can I see?"

Since she didn't think it would hurt anything, she held out her left hand. The elf unhooked a small scanner from their belt and hovered it over her palm. After a moment, there was a low beep. The elf squinted at the screen.

In her work, Carmine had scanned hundreds of ID chips, but it'd never occurred to her to scan her own. The matron got her one when she was fourteen, but seeing as she never left the crypt, she didn't have cause to use it. She'd simply forgotten it was there.

Recalling the hundreds of records she'd pulled up over her career, Carmine wondered what the captain would see there. Vaccination records and birth year, probably. No bank accounts or driver's license. Nothing important.

"Carmine Safi. Current residence is Mooresville, North Carolina, Neutral Zone."

Carmine Safi.

She blinked rapidly. Decades of being told she had no family, no family name, had scrubbed it from her memory, but as soon as it left the captain's lips, she remembered. *Safi.* Her father's family name.

It was a bittersweet thing to remember, and to know that it had been lost for so long, hovering just out of sight. Old grief thumped her hard, right in the center of her chest.

Her gaze wandered over the captain's shoulder, back to Atticus. He was watching her. The unaffected mask was gone. His eyes were wild, his grip on the steering wheel white-knuckled. Those broad shoulders were hiked up to his ears and his dark brows lowered at a sharp angle. He looked like he might leap out of the RV at even the smallest signal of distress.

Carmine shuffled her feet. She wanted to go to him. To tell him her name. Instinct promised her that if she got close enough, the ache in her chest would go away. He'd chase it off somehow. He'd make it all better, then take her away to some place soft and dark and close, where they could indulge in one another forever.

"...certified mortician."

She blinked and forced herself to focus on the captain. "Yes?"

"Is that what you're coming to the EVP for, Miss Safi? Are you looking for a new job?"

She licked her lips. "I... Yes. I want to start a new life here." It was true enough.

The elf clipped their scanner back onto their belt. They took one step closer. Even though they lowered their head, Carmine still had to crane her neck to meet their gaze. "Miss Safi, you can tell me anything right now, okay? I'm not going to judge you or get angry. I'd like you to be honest with me."

"Okay."

"Do you need some help?"

Electricity snapped down her spine and jolted every nerve. Her eyes opened wide. *I could ask for help.*

She looked into the elvish captain's dark gaze and realized she could escape. Right at that moment. She could say yes, tell them everything — that she'd been a blood bride, that she didn't want to be, that all she needed was a chance to live on her own. It was a risk, but was it any bigger than trusting Atticus?

If her heart beat any faster, she thought it'd pop. Just burst like a bloody balloon in her chest.

"If you're in danger, even if you just don't want to be near the man in the RV, I can walk you inside the station over there and you'll never see him again," the captain murmured. "I'll protect you. Make sure you get some help."

You'll never see him again.

The elation crashed, leaving her shaken and a little queasy. She glanced at Atticus again. She didn't think he could hear them, but he seemed to sense something was off anyway. He'd leaned over. His expression was stark, the tendons of his neck pulled taut.

I'd never see him again.

That thing in her screamed so long and loud, it blocked out everything else.

"I'm okay," she heard herself say, from some great distance.

The elf's face creased with worry. "Are you *sure*?"

"Yes." Carmine wiped her sweaty palms on her thighs. Everything was a risk. No one could be trusted. But...

"He's mine. I want to be with him."

"He's yours?"

"He's my anchor," she lied, mostly to herself.

The elf didn't look entirely convinced, but they did take a step back. "I saw a bite, but... Isn't he a vampire?"

"I'm neutral," she replied, glancing around reflexively, like someone might pop out of the woods and snatch her the moment the words left her mouth.

It took a second for the elf to understand what she was saying. "Oh. So you can— *Oh.*" They ran their gloved fingers through the short bristles of their hair. "So he's your consort?"

"My what?"

"Your mate."

"Oh, um..." Carmine brushed her hair over her shoulder, hopefully hiding her blush from everyone, including Atticus. An anchor was supposed to be forever, and in her fantasy she liked the idea of never letting Atticus go, but reality was a different matter. Carefully managed, anchors *could* be temporary, and she and Atticus certainly had no claim on one another. *Especially* after she'd blown whatever chance she had the previous night.

"It's new. Depends on if he wants to be."

The elf made a face. "So odd."

"What is?"

"The idea that you might not know. Or that you might make the wrong choice." They shook their head. "Elves are different."

Carmine blinked owlishly up at them. "Well, you *are* green."

When the elf smiled, they flashed two sets of razor sharp fangs. "You've got me there." They jerked their head toward the RV. "You sure?"

"Yes." *Gods, I hope so.*

"All right then." They stepped aside.

Carmine hustled around them, eager to get back to the relative safety of the RV, but she didn't dare meet Atticus's gaze as she clambered back into the passenger's seat. She'd only just clipped herself in when there was a knock on her window.

When she lowered it, the elf gave her a long look and said, "It was nice chatting with you, Miss Safi. I hope your new life works out. I'm sure you'll find a job as a mortician here. Gods know we need more good people willing to tend to the dead."

Carmine offered her a small smile. "Thank you. For that and — and for the other thing. I really appreciate it."

The elf patted the door. "No worries. Have a good night." They looked past Carmine and nodded. "You drive safe."

Atticus's voice came out a little lower than normal when he replied, "Wouldn't dream of doing anything else."

"And Miss Safi?"

"Yes?"

"You need anything, you go to Patrol. Ask for Captain Bennet. They'll find me. Understood?"

Carmine's throat went tight with gratitude. "Understood."

Chapter Thirteen

"Safi?"

Carmine startled. It was the first word Atticus had spoken to her since they pulled through the gate. It was nearing dawn and they'd pulled off the main road. She assumed the stunning overlook up ahead was where they'd wait for Michael, but he hadn't told her one way or another.

She had to swallow hard before she could reply. "That's my last name."

"I thought you didn't know your last name."

"I couldn't remember it," she replied, unable to parse his tone. Was he angry still? He didn't sound very friendly, but he didn't bark at her, either. "I didn't know it until Captain Bennet scanned my chip."

Atticus still didn't look at her. The corded muscles of his forearms, covered with tattoos and exposed by his t-shirt, strained beneath his skin. He looked like he was holding onto the wheel for dear life as he slowly guided the RV and trailer off the road and onto the overlook.

"What was that about being a mortician?"

Carmine rearranged the folds of her dress over her knees. Her lungs went so tense with panic at the thought of leaving him that she almost couldn't get the words out. "That's what I did for the crypt. I tended the dead. Repaired bodies. Cleaned them. Got them ready for families to sit vigil and then bury them or send them to be cremated at Glory's Temple."

Atticus's jaw worked for a moment before he asked, "Why didn't you tell me that?"

"Um... I thought you would assume that's what I did. I wasn't hiding it."

"Do you like it?"

"Yes?"

"That sounded like a question."

"I'm confused about what's happening right now." She risked another peek at his expression, but it was unchanged. "I love tending the dead. It's my favorite thing."

Second favorite. Now she had a new favorite thing, but she wasn't certain she'd ever be able to do it again. Her stomach cramped at the thought.

"What did Captain Bennet ask about?"

The hair on the back of her neck stood up. Carmine got the distinct impression that she was being tested. Speaking slowly, she answered, "They asked me if I needed help and offered to get me away from you."

Atticus turned his head so fast, she momentarily worried about the integrity of his spinal column. "And you said *no?*"

Carmine's eyes went wide. "Was that wrong?"

He slammed the brake. Luckily they weren't going very fast. She only rocked in her seat a little as he engaged the parking brake and unclipped his seatbelt so fast, the buckle hit the window with a jarring *clack!*

Heart leaping into her throat, she gasped, "What's going—"

She yelped when he reached over the console to unbuckle her. He hooked his hands under her arms and dragged her over the cupholders. She scrambled to accommodate him, not wanting to bang her shins, and before she'd really processed what was happening, she was seated in his lap again.

He keeps doing that, she thought, dazed, as he arranged her legs out over the console.

Cupping the side of her neck, he turned her head to face him with his thumb. "Doll, why didn't you say yes to the elf?"

She found it hard to look at him, so she lowered her gaze to the puncture wounds on his throat. Her hand itched to touch it. Stroke it. Revel in the mark that was hers.

She didn't dare, though. It was one thing to pretend and lie to Captain Bennet, but it was another to endure his rejection again. A cold feeling like dread washed through her at the memory of how he'd set her aside like he couldn't stand to touch her.

She understood that he was right to be angry, but he'd also washed his hands of the moment and what they'd shared so quickly. That hurt worse than anything else.

So she kept her hands tightly clasped in her lap when she answered, "I don't know."

"Why are you lying?"

She lifted a shoulder in a tense shrug. Her reasoning felt ridiculous now. She didn't have logic. Carmine had acted on pure instinct: the one that screamed at her to run back to him.

"Doll." He stroked her cheek with the pad of his thumb. Butterflies exploded into flight in her stomach at that small, gentle touch. "Please look at me."

"No, thank you."

"Why not?"

"You're angry at me."

"I was upset, yeah. Mostly at myself for being a huge fucking asshole and touching you when I shouldn't have."

The words were so sour they almost refused to form, but Carmine forced them out. "Because you didn't want to defile me."

"Fuck. No, Carmine, that's not why I was upset." He dipped his head, probably to catch her eye, but she stubbornly refused to look anywhere but at her bite. Which was a mistake, because it only made her crave him more.

"I was mad because it was— Listen, there are a lot of reasons. First of all, I thought I told you that you don't have to hook up with someone to be safe. It pissed me off to think that you only... that we did that because you felt like you had to, that *I* made you feel that way. That I— gods, that I took advantage of that desperation fucking gutted me. You don't have to trade yourself for anything, and you sure as fuck won't be *defiled* by having sex. That's the second thing: sex is good, Carmine. Fuckin' sacred when it's with the right person, the right time, the right chemistry. It doesn't *ruin* you."

"I didn't think so," she replied, matter-of-fact. She could see now why some people might revere sex — all it took was one orgasm at the hands of her vampire to *get it* — but she'd never believed the moral part of it that the crypt tried to beat into her. It just didn't make sense, not when she saw the cold facts of life and death and bodies on her slab every day.

Sex couldn't have more moral value than any other bodily function, and she didn't feel shame when she peed, so...

Still, that didn't change the fact that *others* valued her perceived purity. "My virginity is a liability."

"How so?"

Exasperated, she finally looked at him. He was very close. Focusing on his cheek instead of the intensity of his eyes, she answered, "If I'm defiled, no groom will want me."

"That's bullshit. Most vampires wouldn't give a shit if you'd had a hundred partners, Carmine. I sure as shit don't."

"But enough *do*," she argued, desperate for him to understand. "My groom does. Anyone who did business with the crypt did. That's enough. If I can ruin myself for even a few grooms, isn't that a good thing?"

Atticus went quiet. When he spoke again, his voice was a croak. "You weren't just trying to buy protection or something?"

"No. I considered it, but that would have been a risk, too. What if I chose wrong? A mate or even just a sexual partner could be just as dangerous as a groom."

Not Atticus, she thought. *I hope.*

His arms circled her, pulled her tight to his chest, and squeezed. "I'm sorry," he grated. "I was hurt. I loved being with you so much that it fuckin' hurt thinking you'd done it because... Whatever. It doesn't matter."

"Oh." Her stomach did a somersault. "I did want to, you know. You didn't take advantage of me. I wanted you to touch me. I... needed it."

"Yeah, you wanted to get rid of your virginity." She felt his chest expand with a huge exhale. "I get it. That was smart, doll."

He's still hurt. That thought sat like a burning coal at the base of her throat.

Carmine pushed at his shoulder, forcing him to let her lean back a little. "Yes, but that's not the *whole* reason."

Atticus had such an intense frown. Everything about him seemed to be turned up to the highest volume at all times. His eyes. His voice. His tattoos. His feelings. She could see the conflict in every line of his expression, and that bothered her.

Reaching up to smooth the lines from his forehead with her fingers, she admitted, "I also just wanted you. I felt safe wanting you, being touched by you. Even if there'd been another person around, I would have chosen you. Is that bad?"

In the moment, she hadn't been thinking of her virginity or its weight. Her ploy had only made it as far as him pulling his collar aside for her to drink. After that, she'd been driven by little more than pure carnal need and *him.*

The tension around his eyes eased. Atticus snagged her wrist. Pressing it to his mouth, he breathed against her fluttering pulse, "No, doll. It's not bad."

He tucked her head into the crook of his neck and held her like that for a while. She didn't complain. All the tense muscles of her body relaxed for the first time since things went sideways. Her eyes grew heavy-lidded. She very subtly turned her nose into his throat and breathed deep, taking the rich scent of him into her body.

The screaming thing in her chest went quiet. *He's so warm. So gentle with me. If I could stay here forever, I would.*

Not because she wanted to change her fate. Not because he'd saved her. Not because she needed a protector.

It was because he felt like home.

Atticus idly brushed his claws through her hair for a while before he asked, "Why didn't you say yes to the elf, doll?"

"I... didn't want to leave you."

A soft puff of air escaped him. Not quite a sigh and not a gasp, but a sound of astonishment nonetheless. "Do you trust me?"

"I think I could."

"That's a start." He turned his head to skim his lips over her forehead. "Everything is gonna be okay, doll."

She let out a sharp exhale before admitting, "I'm scared to go with Michael."

He tensed. "Why?"

"I don't know him." She picked at the fabric of his shirt. "He's not you. When I think about leaving you, it doesn't feel right. Like stepping off a cliff I can't see."

She expected him to immediately reassure her, but he didn't. Instead, he gravely agreed, "You're right. Gods, you're so fuckin' brave, Carmine. So brave. This would scare the shit out of me, too. Being passed around, not sure if anything was true or if I'd end up someplace worse than where I already was. I could be sending you with anyone, to anywhere."

Panic momentarily took hold of her. "Please don't."

Don't lie. Don't break my heart.

Having that tiny bud of trust crushed would be a massive blow. Maybe one she couldn't come back from.

Atticus cupped her cheek. Pulling back a bit, he looked down at her. Perfectly solemn, he promised, "I won't. As much as it kills me to say it, you're going to be safe with Michael. He's a good man. He'll drive you to the estate. Shouldn't take more than three hours, and you'll be safe from the sun in the blacked out backseat. You'll be greeted by Zia and the boss and my sister who are going to stay up to wait for you. Adriana will probably cry. She does that a lot. And then I'll meet you there. Make sure your house is all set up. You'll be safe, Carmine. I won't sleep until you feel it."

"Okay." She let out a shaky breath. "Okay."

He seemed to understand that she wouldn't be able to truly believe it until she saw it all in front of her, real and hers. Eyelids lowering, he murmured, "We have a few minutes before Michael should be here. I don't want you leaving my sight with an empty stomach. You hungry, doll?"

Her belly swooped. "Yes."

Atticus thumbed her lower lip. His touch was featherlight, his eyes dark. "I don't want you being hungry around another man, fucked up as that sounds." He leaned down to bump the tips of their noses together. In a softer, huskier voice, he continued, "I want you to feed from me, doll. Just me."

Peeking through her lashes, she asked a question that had nagged at her, "Do you want to feed from *me*?"

His breath hissed from between his fangs. "You have no fucking idea, but you're not strong enough for that yet." Pressing his thumb into the divot between her lip and chin, he applied gentle pressure until her lips parted. "And I love your bite, doll. I want to feel your fangs one more time before the real world tries to steal you from me."

That was a dangerous game. If he didn't want to be her anchor, then they couldn't do it more than a handful of times. Even two was pushing it. More than that and they ran the risk of her venom taking. Becoming an anchor could be reversed, of course, but venom withdrawal was horrific. Even a temporary anchor suffered when they stopped receiving regular injections.

But she didn't say that. She didn't want to say no, and she didn't want him to be smart. There was every chance that she'd get into Michael's car and she'd never see Atticus again. He could betray her. Michael could betray him. Her groom could snatch her. Anything could happen, and even if it didn't, everything would change once they left the safe bubble of the RV.

In all likelihood, she'd never get a chance to taste him again. Of course she was going to take it.

"Touch me," she whispered, daring to skim her lips against his. His shuddering breath puffed across her mouth. "Please."

This time, when she slid her fangs into the unbitten side of his neck, she did it smoothly, with more anticipation than the nerves that had shaken her the first time. She moaned at the release of venom, the first gush of rich blood into her mouth. She clung to him, stroked his hair and his jaw and the planes of his chest. Her mind drifted into some new, warm place that felt like home.

"That's it," he murmured, gathering her close and sliding a hand under her dress. His callused fingers dipped into her panties, stroking slick flesh with a reverence that took her breath away. "I've got you, doll. I've got you."

For the first time since they met, she let herself believe it.

Chapter Fourteen

"You know, you're really fuckin' lucky."

Atticus shifted his weight on the stiff leather cushion of his chair. His boots left imprints on the fancy rug beneath it, ones he'd have to take care of before he left. He gripped his bolt gun, letting it dangle between his spread thighs. His other hand loosely clasped his wrist.

Across the *big man* desk, strapped to his *big man* chair, Junger moaned. He couldn't scream anymore. Not because he'd run out of steam, but because his vocal chords were beginning to desiccate.

Treating the noise like it was a response, Atticus continued, "You are. See, if I hadn't looked in the trailer, she would have been locked in there for days. A week, almost, sealed up in that tin can with almost no ventilation. And if I found out that she'd been in there the whole time, what's happening right now would have been much, much worse."

He'd done a really good job of banking his rage. He'd focused on getting Carmine safe, taking care of her in the best way he knew how. Yeah, it wasn't perfect and he regretted not having more self-control when she needed it, but he'd gotten the message that she was with Zia and Adriana, so everything worked out.

Atticus liked to think that he wasn't a particularly violent man. He didn't take pleasure in it. He didn't throw things or raise his voice when he got pissed — not that he *could,* what with the damage to his throat, but still. He was an even-keel kind of man, as most hitmen tended to be. To do the work well, you had to be cool. Collected. Removed.

Harlan taught him early on that he couldn't invest himself in the shit they did to survive their world, and when they left the syndicate, he told Atticus to leave it behind.

He had, for the most part. And it wasn't like he missed it. Sure, he was restless and a little bored with his new life, but that was sure as shit better than wondering if he'd end up with a bolt in his brain every time he left the house.

He didn't miss blood feuds and back-stabbings and blackmail, but he was damn glad he'd lived that life when he tailed Junger from the meet-up spot to his gaudy mansion in a rich neighborhood east of Sacramento. Another man would not have understood what to do with the fury that unfurled in him like a coiled snake. A man who'd lived a different life wouldn't have been able to give Junger exactly what he deserved.

It was a thing of beauty, watching the businessman's face go ashen, then puce, when he cracked open the trailer to find nothing. Not even a box.

Atticus hadn't given him a second to reach for his phone. As soon as Carmine's absence registered, he put his gun to Junger's head and marched him into his own house.

That coiled snake didn't listen when Junger began to scream, to bargain, to demand answers and then beg not a moment later as Atticus tore his shirt in two and exposed his pasty belly to the world.

The snake waited, patient and terrible, as Atticus tied him to the chair and set up the lights on his desk. It waited as he donned a pair of sunglasses. It waited as he took his seat, made himself comfortable, and turned the lights on.

And then it struck.

"She's beautiful," he explained as Junger sobbed, his tears nothing but dust in the face of the UV lights slowly frying him. "Biggest blue eyes you ever saw. So expressive. So fuckin' smart. D'you know she has a degree in mortuary science?"

He eyed the blisters that had begun to pop on Junger's jowls. A little sunlight exposure wouldn't kill most fully grown vampires. It was a bit like how one might react to radiation. It was all about how long they were exposed — and at what level.

"How much did you pay for her? Whatever it was, I'm telling you it wasn't enough."

"P-Please turn the lights *off*," he blubbered. "I'll tell you. Anything. Everything. *Please!*"

"You'll tell me what you paid and who paid you?"

"*Yes!*"

Atticus shrugged and levered himself up. His ass was sore from all the driving, not to mention the hour he'd been sitting in that awful chair. *Rich men have the worst fucking furniture.*

Looming over the desk, he hit the button on the tiny remote. Instantly, the over-bright room plunged into darkness. Junger sagged in his chair and began to weep in earnest.

"Hey shithead," Atticus prodded, "numbers. Names. *Now.*"

Junger's voice was barely understandable, but luckily Atticus had plenty of experience parsing agonized, desperate blabber. Junger told him the price. He told him how Carmine was offered at a discount because there was heat on the crypt, how Junger felt like a big man getting a steal on goods so precious. He gave the information on his various hidden bank accounts over, as well as everything else even tangentially related to the sale.

When he had nothing left to give, Junger rasped, "Please, I just wanted an heir. I don't understand what I did to cross you or Mr. Bounds. I'll give you anything. Take her. I won't try to—"

"This isn't about me or Mr. Bounds," he calmly informed him. "And the fact that you haven't even considered that I'm here for *her* is the reason you're sitting in that chair."

Atticus turned the lights back on.

Junger squealed, his whole body jerking reflexively as if he could recoil from the light. "You *said*," he cried, voice cracking. "You promised if I gave you the information you'd stop!"

"I didn't promise shit, motherfucker." He settled back in his chair and checked his phone. A message from Harlan came through.

She's asking about you.

His chest went so damn tight, it was actually hard to breathe for a second.

She had to be so scared. The look in her eyes when he wrapped her in his coat and sent her off with Michael would haunt him for the rest of his life. Carmine had appeared so lost, but she'd looked to *him* for reassurance. For safety. For sustenance. For pleasure.

The bites on his neck throbbed with a deep, pleasant ache. They'd be gone soon. Bites healed fast, what with the coagulant properties of vampire saliva, but the thought didn't make him happy.

For the first time in a long time, Atticus felt the itch to run back home. He needed to see that she was settled with his own eyes. The jealous monster in him howled at the idea of someone else making sure she was fed and comfortable.

It needed her. *Now.*

Atticus leaned back in his chair and held his phone up to his ear. Harlan picked up on the first ring. "You must be almost done."

"Yeah. She okay?"

"Shaken and not very talkative, but fine. She slept in the guest room. She's been hanging out with the girls since she woke up, but the only time she really speaks is when she asks about you. I presume that's nerves."

"She's not used to talking much," he explained, rubbing his chest like it could ease the tender ache there. "Give her a minute and she'll warm up. Zia okay?"

"She's delighted. You know how she loves a full house."

Yeah, he did. Atticus had no doubt that soon enough, there'd be more than just Serafina running around on the estate. Zia loved having all the men over whenever she could, but he knew she wanted her house bursting with more than hardened criminals.

"Atticus," Harlan said, speaking in a low voice that always accompanied a scolding, "Michael said he saw bites."

"He did."

No use denying it. If he'd wanted to hide what they'd done, he would have told her to bite him somewhere else. But as fucked up as the situation was, he didn't want to hide it. He wanted everyone to know that she'd had those pretty fangs in *his* throat.

"So that's how it is."

He breathed past the reflexive, squirming guilt that still lived in his chest. "Yeah, that's how it is."

Atticus's jaw flexed as he watched Junger's head loll against the back of the chair, like he was trying to disconnect it from his body so it could roll away from the lights.

He wasn't sure how he was going to make it work, let alone convince her to give him a chance without implying she needed to in order to earn her place, but Atticus was in too deep to back out now. The moment she chose him over freedom with Captain Bennet, trusted him, there was no going back.

He'd never wanted a blood bride, but he'd do anything for *her*.

"You want to talk to her?"

His heartbeat accelerated. "Yes. Thanks, boss."

"Of course. We'll discuss this more when you get home." There was a pause, then some rustling. Familiar voices came through the connection — Zia's rapid-fire speech, Serafina's babble, and Adriana's gentle response to something.

Distantly, he heard Harlan announce, "Carmine, it's Atticus. He wants to speak—"

There was an abrupt sound as the phone was jostled before

Carmine's high voice came through, demanding, "Are you coming back?"

Atticus closed his eyes, savoring the sweetness of her voice. There was no guile, no shyness. Just an earnest desire to know when he'd be home.

Maybe she still worried that he'd break his word to her, but he chose to believe she just wanted to see him again.

"I'm almost done here, doll," he answered. "You doing okay? Did Michael behave?"

"I'm fine." She hesitated, making him tense, before she added, "And Michael was fine, but I don't think we're compatible. I prefer you."

Thank fuck. I love how she never sugarcoats shit. Swiping his palm over his mouth, he muttered, "Well, good. Need me to pick up anything on my way back?"

He'd already planned on grabbing her a phone, but he knew she needed more. Not just essentials, but every little thing he took for granted, like knick-knacks and a favorite shampoo and decorations for her room. Gods, she didn't even have real *clothes.*

"Zia and Adriana want to take me shopping," she replied in a lower voice, her unease bleeding through.

"Do you want to do that? You don't have to, doll. They can grab stuff for you if you give them your sizes. Or I can do it. Whatever you're comfortable with."

"I want to go." There was a pause, then, in the no-nonsense tone she used whenever she was trying to cover up her nerves, she added, "But I don't have any money, and I don't want anyone to pay for my things. I need a job. How soon can I start looking for a funeral home?"

He didn't bother explaining to her that he was more than happy to cover anything she needed — up to and including giving her his blood — because he understood that might make her feel even more beholden to them. Instead, he assured her, "We'll look into the job thing when you're settled. In the meantime, don't worry about money. Turns out your groom wanted to make things right. He gave you the price he paid the crypt and a bit more on top. My friend Tarrence is gonna transfer it into an account for you tonight."

Across the desk, Junger went very still, then began to thrash. Atticus imagined he would have screamed in protest if there'd been any moisture left in his throat.

"Why would he do that?"

"Because, dollface," he answered, flicking the lights onto their highest setting, "he's very, very sorry."

Chapter Fifteen

The manor was bursting with life when Atticus pulled down the long, winding driveway.

His heart jammed itself in his throat as he pushed the car door open. The lights were on in the house, turned low for sensitive vampire eyes. The glow shimmered in the thick, diamond panels of the old glass as he jogged up the brick steps to the front door.

The manor was two hundred years old and boasted a heavy, forest green door. A massive arch of roses hung over the entrance, almost obscuring all the brickwork some master mason had painstakingly crafted. Since Zia and Harland got together, a lot of the estate had become wild with life and color — a marked change from the strict orderliness the boss had always demanded. Normally Atticus felt a small squeeze of tenderness whenever he looked at the wild, towering rose bush, but not that night.

Being family, he could have barged right in. He wanted to. But instinct held him back. This was another vampire's domain, and as much as it pissed him off that Carmine was inside, Atticus didn't love the idea of Harlan throwing him out a window for startling his family.

Biting the insides of his cheeks so hard he tasted copper, Atticus banged the meat of his palm on the door and waited.

C'mon, he thought, shifting his weight from foot to foot. *Hurry up!*

The heavy door swung open on silent hinges. Harlan stood in the doorway, his long, gray-streaked hair loose. He was dressed as casually as he ever got outside of workout gear: a pristine white button down, slacks, and a wristwatch worth more than the manor on his wrist.

Harlan Bounds was a man obsessed with the finer things in life, which explained why he had his two year old daughter perched on his hip.

Serafina had inherited her mother's round cheeks, cleft chin, and penchant for babbling, but she had Harlan's intensity. That intensity wasn't diminished by her cuteness, nor by the fact that her wispy hair was gathered into a palm tree on the crown of her head. Both chubby hands clutched her miniature bottle of synth, specially calibrated for growing vampires, when she fixed her dark eyes on Atticus.

For just a moment, she gave him a look of such profound shock and hurt that he almost took a reflexive step back. And then she exploded.

"Atty!" she wailed, lunging for him so fast that Harlan had to move with her, lest she pitch herself out of her father's arms.

There was a messy hand-off as Harlan extracted the bottle from her hands and Atticus fumbled to get her securely in his arms. Serafina sobbed with huge, pitiful tears.

"She missed you," Harlan dryly noted. He stepped back, allowing Atticus to cross the threshold. "You're not allowed to leave again."

"I missed you, too," Atticus assured the toddler, stroking her back as she clung to him. As much as he wanted to charge through the house to find Carmine, he took his time giving her a tight hug.

It wasn't the first time Serafina exploded in a fit of emotion — something he was certain she picked up from Zia's side of the family — but he was horrified to have been the cause for tears.

She railed at him in her high-pitched, gasping babble. It was impossible to understand her, but he got the gist of it. He'd messed up and she wanted him to know it.

Luckily her fit only lasted a few minutes before she was back to her normal bubbly self. Atticus brushed the tears from her chubby cheeks as she pulled back to yammer at him, telling him some grand story he could only partially comprehend.

"Atty bite?" He blinked, taken off-guard when she stopped mid-sentence to point a chubby finger at his neck. "*Baba* bite?"

Baba was the Turkish word for father, like *anne* was the word for mother, and what Serafina called Harlan about fifty percent of the time. Daddy was used whenever she really wanted something. The strategy had a very high success rate.

It took him a second to process her question. Blanching, he stammered, "Ah, no, Fina. That's…"

"That's Carmine's bite," Harlan bluntly explained, handing the bottle back to his daughter. "I only bite your mother, princess, just like *you* will only bite *your* anchor someday. Some very, very distant day."

A flush crawled up Atticus's neck to sear his ears. He had no idea why. He wasn't ashamed of Carmine's bite — far from it — but something about the situation made him feel a bit like he'd been caught with his hand in the cookie jar. Harlan had been blasé on the phone, but what would he really think about Atticus pursuing a blood bride?

Harlan's opinion was the one he respected most in the world. If he disapproved, if he thought Atticus should back off…

I can't. I won't.

"Where is she?" he croaked.

Harlan tilted his head in the direction of the kitchen. "The girls are doing a makeover."

"*Anne's* haircut," Serafina chirped before taking a noisy slurp of her synth.

Atticus's brow furrowed. "Haircut?"

A hint of a smile curved Harlan's lips. "My anchor thinks that because she trims my hair, she can handle Carmine's." He shrugged. "I'll pay to have it fixed."

"See!" Serafina squirmed so violently that Atticus was forced to hastily lower her to the floor. She scampered off on socked feet, her palm tree ponytail bobbing.

"Walk," Harlan called after her. "And careful with your synth, princess."

Atticus made to follow her, but he was stopped by a hand on his shoulder. Harlan fixed him with a familiar, scrutinizing look when he said, "Tell me what's going on."

Harlan Bounds was an old-school vampire. Raised in the vicious, dog-eat-dog world of the Amauri crime family, he was taught early on to never ask for something when it could be demanded instead. To the soft, polite people of the EVP, Harlan was as hard and rude as they came.

But for Atticus, there was a lot of comfort in the directness with which his adopted father spoke. He and Carmine were similar in that way. Harlan could always be trusted to say what was on his mind, and he never hesitated to act when he deemed it necessary. He was steady. When Atticus needed to lean on someone, Harlan was there, as strong and dependable as steel.

He didn't even know how to explain the enormity of the thing inside of him, let alone the complexity of it, so instead Atticus rasped, "I want her."

"You don't seem overjoyed by that."

"No, I am. She's perfect. I..." He rubbed the tense muscles of his nape. "There's nothing I don't like about her. I'm fuckin' obsessed with her, boss. But she's a bride."

Harlan's expression didn't change. "Not anymore."

A vicious stab of pleasure struck him. *That's right,* he thought, the fingers of his right hand curling into a fist. *Junger's dead.*

But the pleasure of that knowledge was short-lived. Atticus squeezed his neck again, saying, "She's venom neutral."

"Obviously."

"I feel so guilty. She's— Isn't it weird? That I'd want her when I've spent my whole life trying to protect Adriana from being a vampire's mate? Doesn't that make me a bad person?"

It was only then that Harlan's expression changed. He arched a dark brow. "That's not what you've protected Adriana from, boy." Atticus opened his mouth to object, but Harlan beat him to it. "It's not. We didn't leave the syndicate life to protect your sister from finding a mate. We left because we wanted her to have the *choice.*"

That was true enough, but it didn't make a dent in the guilt that sat heavy and thick inside him. He wanted her so bad it made him ache, and he knew he was in too deep to back out now, but... "What if Carmine doesn't feel like she *has* a choice?"

He was fucking haunted by the memory of her bite, but also by the whiplash of horror and shame he felt when he realized the intimacy they'd shared had been a ploy. The idea that Carmine might feel like she *had* to return his advances, even subconsciously, ate him up like acid.

Harlan's brow inched a little higher. "It's interesting that you think I'd let you get away with that."

"Boss..."

"You want her to be your anchor." It wasn't a question, and neither was the statement that followed. "You want to be *her* anchor."

His throat felt like it was closing in on itself, but he managed to choke out, "Yeah, I think I do."

"There's no *I think* in that scenario. You've got to figure that shit out and be one hundred percent sure," Harlan commanded, just as serious as he was when he held a life in his hands. "When you do, then you treat her like you would any other potential anchor."

Atticus's heart lurched. "How do I make sure she wants me back? Really wants me?"

"I don't know," Harlan replied, eyes gleaming with dark humor, "maybe date and shit."

A startled laugh burst out of him. That was the exact piece of advice he gave Harlan when he was attempting to woo Zia, his employee at the time, and it was about as helpful for him as it was for Atticus — which wasn't very helpful at all.

"Are you enjoying this?"

"A little." He paused before blandly adding, "Have you considered buying her a car?"

"I don't think she has a driver's license. If she did, I'm pretty sure she would have stolen the RV."

"That would've been smart."

"Carmine's super smart," he replied, smiling like the besotted idiot he was. "Did she tell you she's a mortician?"

"She mentioned something about needing to find a morgue. Glad to know it was for strictly professional reasons."

A squeal of child's laughter echoed down the hall. The house was a warren of short doorways and interconnected rooms, meaning sound didn't carry very well. For Serafina's laughter to have reached them all the way by the front door, it had to have been explosive — and par the course for the little vampire.

Like bees to honey, both men were drawn toward the joyous sound. The closer they got to the kitchen, the easier it was for Atticus to pick up on the scent of cherries buried beneath the comforting smells of the home and its occupants.

His heart thudded unevenly against his ribs as he stepped into the kitchen and took in the scene.

Carmine sat in a wooden chair in the middle of the room, her back to him. She was dressed in some clothing he vaguely recognized as Adriana's, with Serafina perched on her lap, her back arched over one of Carmine's arms so that her little head dangled upside down.

Adriana, her wavy auburn hair pulled up into a bun and dressed in her usual sweater and jeans combination, was wiping what appeared to be splatters of Serafina's synth from a cabinet. Buzzing around them was Zia, her extravagant curls gleaming in the low light and a pair of slim silver scissors in her hand.

On the floor, coiled like a winding river of ink, was Carmine's hair.

Adriana noticed him first. She looked up from her task and locked eyes with him. For a moment, the world went still. Atticus braced for her judgment, her disgust that he'd preyed on a vulnerable blood bride, but it didn't come. She took one look at the bites on his neck, pointed, and instantly began to guffaw.

"I knew it," she wheezed, slapping the tips of her fingers against the counter. "I *knew* it! Zia, you owe me a girl's night!"

"What? How can you possibly— Oh!" Zia turned, as did every other head in the room. She took a long look at his neck. A wide, mischievous grin dimpled her cheeks. "Welcome home, Atty! It looks like your vacation agreed with you. Look at him, Adriana, he's practically *glowing*."

His cheeks were hot and he couldn't tell if he was relieved by their reaction or annoyed, but none of that mattered when Carmine craned her neck to look at him.

Zia'd cut most of her hair off, leaving it a glossy, shoulder-length fall of blue-black. He couldn't say it was skillfully done, but he liked the way the ends curled around her neck and jaw, framing the delicate features of her face rather than hiding them.

And it was a thing of profound beauty, watching the way her eyes went huge and dark when they fixed on him. Almost like she didn't mean to say it, Carmine whispered, "You came back."

He was moving, but he didn't make the decision to do it. His body acted on its own, forcing him to cross the short distance between them at a pace that was by no means casual.

"'Course I did," he replied, laying one palm on Serafina's head while his other hand sought out the shorn ends of Carmine's hair. "You look so fuckin' pretty, doll."

"Language, Mr. Caldwell!" Zia snipped her scissors at him. The rose-shaped marriage sigil between her brows, the very same one Harlan sported, crinkled with displeasure. "There are impressionable young minds in the room."

He tossed the witch an apologetic smile. *To think there was a time when she was scared of me.*

"My bad, Mrs. Bounds. It won't happen again."

She rolled her eyes. "Yes, it will."

"Probably."

"You shouldn't swear around children," Carmine told him, as prim as a schoolmistress. "It's not good for their development."

"Atty's first word was *shit,*" Adriana chimed in, sounding far too pleased to relay that particular tidbit. "And his second was *head.*"

Carmine's eyes, so big and blue in her face, went wide. "It was?"

Atticus shot his sister a glare. "It's what our mom called our dad. It isn't my fault I thought that was his name."

"Charming," Harlan muttered.

"It's better than Adriana's."

Carmine leaned closer and whispered, "What was Adriana's?"

Taking any opportunity to get closer to her, Atticus pressed his lips to her ear and murmured, "Piss."

A laugh, sweet and clear, bubbled out of her. Something in Atticus's chest swelled, made him straighten up and push his shoulders back. *Pride.* He was damn proud to have made his suspicious, wily little vampire *laugh.*

"Was it really?"

"No," he admitted, grinning, "it was Atty."

"That's much nicer." She hesitated a moment before whispering, "Do you really like my hair? It feels strange."

"I'm sure it does," he replied, thumbing the line of her jaw, "but it's gorgeous, doll. You're gorgeous."

Her gaze searched his for a long moment before she nodded once, decisively. "Did... Did the other thing go okay?"

Aware of Serafina's nearness — hard to miss when tiny fingers were rooting through his pockets — Atticus leaned in close again. "He's dead. You never have to worry about him or anyone else again."

Carmine sucked in a sharp breath. "Will you get in trouble?"

"Nah. Remember when I told you I was a hunter?"

"Yes."

"I didn't just find people, and I was very, very good at my job."

Carmine's expression was inscrutable when she asked, "Is that still your job?"

Do you still kill people?

He knew the question was coming. Atticus had never hidden his intentions for Junger from her, but it was one thing to hear a threat and quite another to know he'd follow through. Now she had to face the reality of what he'd been, what he was, and who he could be.

He felt a bit like they were standing on the edge of something, a perilous but unseen cliff. "No," he murmured, stomach swooping, "not unless someone I care about is threatened."

For one agonizing moment, he was certain he'd plunged off the cliff alone, but when Carmine tilted her head into his touch, he knew she'd jumped with him. "I can live with that."

Knees practically gone to jelly, he breathed, "Good."

"So... I'm free?"

Unable to resist her pull, Atticus pressed a reverent kiss to the shell of her ear. "You're free, doll."

"Thank you. For all of this. For everything." She paused, and for a moment they existed in their own tiny little world. One that was just them, just the way they looked at each other, the way gravity itself felt different when they breathed the same air. "Why didn't you tell me Adriana was like me?"

Skimming the very tips of his fingers over the jut of her chin, he answered, "That's her secret to share, not mine."

"It might have made me trust you faster if you'd told me."

"Maybe, but it still wouldn't have been right."

Carmine's lashes lowered, obscuring his view of her eyes, when she touched the back of his tattooed hand. He sucked in a breath, rocked by the feeling of her smooth skin on his scarred knuckles. "I would have trusted you faster... but I trust you more because you didn't."

Chapter Sixteen

It didn't take too long for someone to find Junger's body. The news chalked it up to malfunctioning auto-blinds. He'd been working late. He probably didn't notice when the blinds never came down to block out the rising sun. A freak accident, Patrol called it.

It was pure coincidence that news about a busted blood bride ring in Mooresville broke the very same day. Whatever attention the story about a local synth manufacturer dying a freak death might have garnered went up in smoke.

Atticus didn't offer any details on what happened to Junger, but he did say his only regret was that he wouldn't be able to give a similar ending to the rest of the crypt's staff, but he reassured her with a reminder that life in a New Zone prison was in many ways a worse fate than death.

No one on Empire Estate seemed even a little bit worried that he'd be blamed for the murder, so Carmine did her best to put aside her worry over it. She didn't feel guilt for his death, though Grim probably wouldn't look approvingly on her for it, but the thought of Atticus suffering any consequences for seeking justice on her behalf made her stomach curdle.

As with all things, however, the sharpest edge of those worries dulled over time. She still thought of it from time to time, but other things took its place in the forefront of her mind.

For two weeks, she existed on a tightrope of anxiety as she navigated a new world. When she wasn't sweating at the idea of it all being a trap — or worse, a dream — she fumbled around trying to figure out how to interact with the people who called the estate home.

Carmine thought Atticus was incredibly chatty, but she soon learned that compared to nearly everyone else, he was actually reserved. Compared to *Zia*, Harlan's greenwitch anchor and mother to little Serafina, he was downright taciturn.

Harlan was similarly quiet, though he could be prompted to speak with only minimal prodding from his anchor. When he did, everyone stopped to listen. Carmine had initially found him stern and intimidating, a little like the High Priest of the crypt, but the more time she spent in the Bounds household, the more she came to appreciate his quiet presence, his thoughtfulness.

Adriana was somewhere between Atticus and Zia. She liked to chat, but she had no problem with long silences, nor with the moments when Carmine said the wrong thing — an all too common occurrence. While Zia's warmth was contagious, Carmine struggled to find her footing in conversation with her and generally preferred to sit back, letting the tide of her enthusiasm sweep her away into an ocean of comfort. Atticus's sister paused much more often, allowing Carmine to work up the nerve to say something.

She quickly came to admire both women — Zia for her overflowing kindness and generosity, and Adriana for her fearless gentleness. Carmine followed them, learned from them, and whispered prayers for the Merciful One to keep them safe, to keep them close. She'd never had friends before, not *really*, so she thanked the gods every dawn for every moment she stole with them.

And then there were the men. The very, very scary men.

She saw them most often in and around the guardhouse by the gate, but many of the men Harlan employed lived in stone cottages like the one she'd been given. They were mostly vampires — New Zone residents, she'd first gathered by their very particular way of speaking — but a few, like Michael the quiet, attentive demon, were other beings. A few sturdy-looking arrants. A lone gargoyle she only ever caught glimpses of. There was even a lynx shifter.

Atticus introduced her to them, explaining that they guarded the estate and would keep her safe, but something in his tone made it clear he'd be keeping a careful eye on them, which for some reason seemed to amuse the group more than anything. Only Michael remained grim-faced, his nod of acknowledgement solemn. Carmine had only been able to make the briefest eye contact before she turned toward Atticus and pressed her face into his shoulder, her face hot from all the attention. She'd abandoned her veil and still tended to forget that there was no curtain of hair at the ready, so she often turned to Atticus to hide away from the world.

In most ways, living on the estate was a dream, but that didn't mean there weren't struggles.

She felt too exposed all the time, too vulnerable. The learning curve for living outside the crypt was far steeper than anything she could have imagined. She often found herself frustrated at her own ignorance, at her awkwardness and fumbling with things that seemed to come so naturally to everyone else. Carmine privately grappled with the shocking amount of autonomy she had, too. Some days she loved her shorn hair, her new clothes, and other days she stared at them both like they belonged to someone else.

The freedom to do anything, to change any part of herself she wished, was by turns intoxicating and terrifying.

The only time she ever felt truly relaxed and comfortable in her own skin was when she was with Atticus. He never coddled her or became annoyed with her missteps. He simply gave her the tools to figure life out on her own, and when she needed help he was there, steady and calm, with a ready smile and a wink.

Among the myriad of everyday things he guided her through, Atticus taught her how to use her new cell phone, and he took her into town to register her new residence. That simple task she'd never even considered left her crying quietly all the way back to the estate.

It wasn't the little packet with information on how her EVP residence application process would work, nor the fact that Atticus had confidently written down her home address as that of the estate that made her so emotional. It was the fact that she was no longer a ghost.

She existed on paper. She was going to be a citizen of the Elvish Protectorate. If she went missing or needed help or wanted to get a driver's license, it would be noticed by *someone*. Because she'd be a person, not just an acolyte or a bride hidden away in the bowels of a crypt, with neither rights nor money nor even her own name.

She was finally *real.*

Atticus could barely get the words out of her, but he managed to piece it all together after he pulled over and held her by the side of the road for a while. He'd gone all mean and angry on her behalf again, but his hands were so gentle as they rubbed her back, touched the blunt ends of her hair, and wiped away her tears.

"I'd kill them all if I could," he told her, "but since that's not an option, I'm going to settle for making sure you get every damn good thing in life."

She was too terrified of jinxing it to say so, but Carmine thought that he'd already given her everything she could have dreamed of.

Well... mostly everything.

He hadn't claimed her.

It hadn't bothered her too much at first. Adjusting to life outside the crypt had been so overwhelming that every other need had been briefly muted. Every day she felt as though she was fighting to survive some hidden test. Spending time with Adriana and Zia helped, and so did knowing that Atticus's cottage was a very short walk through the woods from hers.

Carmine was never alone for those first few weeks, and having a fellow bride nearby helped her confidence flourish. The fact that Adriana was allowed to come and go freely — even live on her own in a city! — was mind-boggling. They'd often stayed up late into the morning discussing their lives, and Adriana had even gone so far as to invite her to live in the city with her.

At any other time, Carmine would have leapt at the chance. Living with a *friend* in a glamorous city like San Francisco was a scenario straight out of her wildest fantasies.

But Atticus wasn't in San Francisco, and when she imagined leaving him behind, that ugly, screaming feeling from her encounter with the Patrol captain returned with a vengeance. Not to mention the way she broke out into a cold sweat at the thought of trying to learn how to function in a place crammed cheek to jowl with people.

Saying no was automatic, instinctual. Adriana didn't look the least bit surprised, but she gently explained that the offer would always be open to her, no matter what happened.

When she left, Carmine was filled with a mixture of anxiety and excitement. She didn't like how empty the cottage felt, but something about being alone felt like an opportunity — a big, open space that was just waiting to be filled with *him*.

Atticus was almost always nearby, hovering at her elbow or driving her places like the registration office for her interview or the local funeral home to inquire about a job. He texted her at dusk and at dawn. He kept careful track of how much she drank, and urged her to spend time with Zia, Harlan, and little Serafina when he was busy.

He was always present, always careful and kind and steady in his growly way, but he wasn't hers. Not completely.

While Adriana stayed on the estate, Carmine's feedings were discreet. After she left, they became more frequent, often ending not only with an orgasm but with her spending the day in his bed or vice versa.

They didn't talk about how they'd long ago crossed the line. They didn't speak about the fact that he was her anchor, that her venom flowed through his veins. He never brought up how bad withdrawal would be, nor even mentioned the fact that he'd begun taking supplements that would allow her to feed from him without worrying about depleting his vital nutrients.

When they were alone together, Carmine was the happiest she'd ever been. She loved the taste of him, the sound of his laugh, and how he introduced her to sexual pleasure. He loved to put on a show for her, drop to his knees, and eat her out on his couch. Sometimes he'd crawl into her bed at dawn and demand she feed while he slid his hand between her thighs, sending her off to sleep with her fangs in his throat and an orgasm singing in her nerves.

He kissed her. He encouraged her to feed. He stood proudly when Zia commented on how healthy Carmine had begun to look, with her shiny hair, her fuller cheeks, and her eyes brighter than they ever had been.

At first, it was perfect. If he'd asked anything more from her during those first weeks, Carmine would have become even more overwhelmed and uncertain of her place. But as time went on, she started to wonder *why* he never took more, like she'd been told to expect.

When a vampire, a groom, claimed her, there would be no guessing, no hesitation. They *took*. They drank and they fucked and they bred.

But he didn't.

He never asked her to reciprocate sexual favors. He never even hinted about wanting a child. Most critically, Atticus never once tried to bite her.

Not when he had his head between her thighs, his fangs mere inches from lush veins. Not when she lay prone and sated from an orgasm beneath him. Not when she silently begged him to.

Her instincts didn't know what to make of it. On one hand, he was her anchor. Her venom coursed through his veins, making his blood even sweeter on her tongue. Her bites decorated his throat, his chest, even his arms. He'd begun to smell a bit like her, her claim permeating all the way through his pores.

On the other hand, she found herself disoriented by *his* lack of claim. She'd made her mark on him, but he hadn't done the same with her. Something that would have been a relief not too long ago now left her anxious and confused. In the RV he'd said he wanted to bite her, but his behavior since then implied the opposite.

What had at first unsettled and confused her had begun to fill her with cold dread — the very same kind she felt whenever she realized she'd made a critical social error or forgot to clean something in the morgue.

Confronting him about it wasn't an option when she feared it would push him away. Carmine knew she couldn't ask Zia, Adriana, or Harlan about the situation, so she'd turned to her old friend: covert research. The answers she'd turned up hadn't reassured her.

Her exact situation wasn't common, but the advice she'd found on mates reluctant to make a claim made her go from cold to downright frigid. As one helpful magazine article said, *"The bottom line is, if he really wanted you, you wouldn't be reading this article. Sorry, babe."*

All the signs pointed to him not wanting her the same way she grew to want him, but why then would he feed her? Touch her? The uncertainty was agony, but the suspicion she'd begun to nurse was worse.

He feels like he has to.

Logically, she understood that Atticus was a good man with a good heart who'd seen a woman in need of help. He'd rescued her and, when she couldn't feed herself properly, he'd offered himself. The arousal he'd clearly experienced was simple biology, which she understood better than most. He'd made no promises, nor declared any feelings for her.

Which was good, because she'd never wanted to be a vampire's bride in the first place. Knowing that Atticus didn't want her shouldn't have slowly strangled the life out of her.

But it did.

~

"Are you nervous?"

"Yes," she answered, smoothing her sweaty palm over her short hair again. Carmine wanted to say more, but she knew it was best to stick to monosyllables when they were in the car. She had to be very careful how much of his scent she breathed in, and that made conversation difficult.

In an effort to gently wean them off each other, Carmine had begun stretching out the time between her feedings. She tried to stay busy, to time things so they conflicted with his schedule, and forcing herself to take sips of synth on nights when they didn't see each other. This was the longest she'd gone since that first bite, and the craving was brutal.

He had to notice that she wasn't feeding as often, but Atticus hadn't said anything. He watched her closely, though, with a furrowed brow and lips pressed thin. Truthfully, she wanted *him* to ask, to notice. The fact that he said nothing only reinforced the fact that things weren't as they should be.

He cut her a glance as he expertly navigated his sleek car around a bend in the mountain road. He looked painfully serious when he reminded her, "If anything happens that you don't like, you call me. I'll come get you."

And fix the issue, she silently finished. The weight of guilt pressed in on her lungs. *Just like you fix everything.*

"Doll."

She unglued her tongue from the aching roof of her mouth. Putting pressure on her venom gland helped with the discomfort a little, but she knew he expected an answer. "I'll call if I have any problems."

"Good. I'm sure it'll go great, though. I'm picking you up at three, and then I'm taking you out to celebrate."

Carmine dared to glance at him. A painful jolt rattled her chest whenever she looked at him for too long, but she just couldn't help herself. "Where?"

He shot her a wolfish smile. "It's a surprise, doll."

She had to look away from his smile. The sight of his fangs, the way his eyes crinkled, the pure joy he radiated... Adriana had off-handedly complained about how stoic her brother was, but Carmine didn't see it. Sure, he often wore a still, borderline surly expression, but to her, he was always so *alive*.

Tucking her hands under her thighs so she didn't reach for him, she nodded. "Okay."

"You're not gonna try and guess?"

"No."

"Why? That's half the fun."

She had to suck in a breath. It burned all the way down her throat, so rich and delicious that it was a shock to her system. Her stomach, full of sour synth she forced herself to drink, cramped painfully. "You won't tell me."

"Well, no, but you could still try."

"I don't know any places to even guess," she reminded him. Seeing the way he winced made her tack on, "Um, a movie? Zia mentioned that you can see them in town, not just in a house."

His wince faded and was replaced by sharp interest. "Do you *want* to see a movie? There are a couple of old-fashioned theatres in Sacramento I can take you to. Not tonight, because there won't be enough time before sunrise, but soon, if you want."

She had only vague ideas about what going to a theatre entailed, but he seemed so keen on the idea that she didn't dare simply shrug. "That sounds fun."

He nodded. "Good. Yes. We'll go, then."

Silence blanketed them. It wasn't as comfortable as it used to be. She hated that.

Atticus cleared his throat. "Is everything okay? You seem..."

She forced a smile. "I'm okay. Just tired."

"You didn't sleep well?" His shoulders tensed. "Is it because you were alone? I'm sorry I didn't join you yesterday. We're over-hauling some of the security systems and I ended up working late. The sun was up by the time I finished, so I slept in the guard house."

"It's fine," she stressed, hoping he could see she was sincere. "Really, Atticus. It's not your fault. You have more important things to do."

"No, I don't. It's my job to take care of you," he argued. "You always sleep well when I'm there, so I've gotta be there."

It's my job to take care of you.

That frigid feeling settled into her bones. It was cold outside, the world dusted in a thin layer of snow, but in her heart there was nothing but brittle ice.

It was a relief when he dropped her off at the funeral home for her first night of work as an assistant mortician. Part of her was always desperate for an escape from the visceral craving she felt when they were together, but the bigger, louder part of her screamed in mourning when he skimmed his knuckles over her cheek and wished her luck.

Not for the first time, she wondered, *How long can I do this?*

She didn't want to leave the estate, but if the craving never went away, she feared Atticus would continue this farce indefi-nitely. Or worse. Maybe someday soon he'd gently, carefully break the news to her that their relationship had to end. He wouldn't force her to leave, but the humiliation of wanting another vampire — bad enough on its own — only to have him indulge her out of misplaced obligation, would destroy the precious new world she'd become so attached to.

That world wasn't just him, but she couldn't pretend that he wasn't at the heart of it.

Tucking her lower lip between her teeth, she hiked her bag higher on her shoulder and forced herself to climb the steps into Pineridge's only funeral home. *This is what I love to do,* she reminded herself as she gripped the shiny brass door knob, *and this is the way I can build my own life, with or without Atticus.*

Even if she really, really didn't want to.

CHAPTER SEVENTEEN

OF COURSE, ATTICUS PICKED HER UP AT THREE ON THE dot. Circling around the car to open her door, he demanded, "How was it? Did everything go okay?"

"It was good. Director Martin is nice."

He'd asked her to call him Jeff, but she'd been way too nervous to take him up on it. Jeff Martin was an elderly vampire who'd run the tiny, mostly-secular funeral home for over two hundred years. He said his children had no interest in helping out with the business, so it was a delight to bring her on board. Jeff talked a lot, smelled like stale synth, and desperately needed help with organization, but she liked him.

Being back amongst the dead was centering. They expected nothing from her. They didn't inspire a dizzying array of conflicting feelings. Tending to them had briefly washed her clean of the worries and hurt that plagued her. She found peace in tending to them, as she always had. It was a quiet, glowing sort of joy that suffused her when she cleaned bloated limbs, combed disheveled hair, and murmured the Merciful Parting in their ear before she draped them in their shrouds.

She treated each one like they were her family, because she

never knew if hers was the last touch, the final kindness they'd ever receive.

But her shift was over, and as soon as she stepped out the door to find Atticus leaning against his car, everything she'd avoided thinking about rushed back. Carmine nervously pushed her hair behind her ear and shuffled by him, careful not to give into the temptation to brush her arm against his chest.

In a bid to regain some of her badly shaken confidence before he arrived, it sounded like a good idea to break out the tiny makeup kit Zia had helped her put together. She'd swiped on some of her glittery eyeshadow in the bathroom before he arrived, but now she felt silly and could barely face him as she slid into the seat.

She'd been very careful not to overdo it. Zia taught her how to highlight her features without overwhelming them, which was exactly what Carmine wanted. Sometimes she missed her ceremonial makeup and mask it provided, but mostly she just wanted to feel pretty. To *sparkle,* even when it felt like her heart was being squeezed tighter and tighter.

Carmine tucked her knees in close together and waited for Atticus to close the door, but when he took a beat longer than usual, she couldn't help but glance up.

He stared at her, one hand curled over the top of the door with a white-knuckled grip, and rasped, "Did you put glitter on?"

Carmine hunched her shoulders and turned away. One hand came up automatically to swipe at her eyelid. "Um, no, it's just—"

Warm fingers curled around her wrist, stopping her from scrubbing off the rest of her eyeshadow. "Hey, no, doll. Stop, please."

She couldn't look at him, let alone speak, so Carmine kept her face turned away. It didn't do a lick of good when he gripped her chin and turned her head toward him. "You didn't have that on when I saw you earlier," he murmured. "I'd remember."

"You said we were going somewhere after work. I wanted to look nice."

Carmine peeked through her lashes. His jaw was tense, his body rigid as he stooped to speak to her.

"You look fuckin' gorgeous," he rasped.

Her heart leapt. "I... It's the one you bought me. The pink."

She had no idea what she planned to say, but it didn't matter anyway. Atticus stole her ability to speak with a fierce kiss. It didn't last long, but it didn't need to. When he pulled back and licked his lips, yearning left nothing but scorched earth in its wake.

His smile was slow and hungry. "Had to check that you're using the lip gloss I got you, too."

When he looked at her like that, *kissed her* like that, it was hard not to have hope. Just a little. Just enough.

The surprise was a trip to a wonderland of light, noise, scents, and sights. It was an *arcade* — one that catered to nocturnal beings and, on Monday nights, to adults only.

Carmine stood in the doorway, clutching Atticus's callused hand as she stared out at the sea of flashing neon lights, squealing machines, and adults meandering around with alcoholic beverages in their hands. It wasn't all vampires, but night owls of every variety that hollered at prize machines and made fools of themselves on light up dance pads.

Giving her a look of concern, Atticus asked, "Is this too much? We can leave if you—"

"No!" She squeezed his hand and tried to catch her breath. It wasn't easy when excitement made it feel a bit like she was standing outside of her own body. "Atty, I want to try *everything.*"

A startled laugh bubbled out of him. Dragging her inside, he announced, "I need some synth first, before you run me ragged."

The reminder that he still wasn't drinking from her made her smile falter, but Carmine quickly covered it by gawking at a claw machine full of electronics.

The bartender offered her a bottle of alcoholic synth, but she turned it down. She and Adriana had some before she left for San Francisco — and drunkenly redecorated Harlan's office with a similarly mulled wine-drunk Zia — but Carmine wasn't about to risk becoming tipsy around *him*. Atticus abstained, too. Loosely cradling his bottle of regular synth between his thumb and forefinger, guided her onto the game floor.

It was *marvelous*.

The excess, the light and sound of the machines, the thumping music playing from the speakers over their heads... Carmine was terrible at every game she tried, but she loved the chaos of it all.

They roared with laughter when they attempted a dance game. Atticus won her a large packet of glowing plastic jewelry from a shooting game, which she donned immediately, and she even managed to get tenth place in a racing car game.

They bounced from one end of the room to the other, doing whatever caught her fancy. Atticus's usual intense expression had been left in the car. Instead, he grinned so wide that his cheeks creased, and when she finally won her first ball rolling game, he whooped and twirled her around until she screamed with laughter.

But that was how it was when they were together. When she wasn't trying to hold her breath, her mind and heart torn in two directions, being with Atticus was effortless. He teased her. He listened to her when she spoke and he snuck small, tender touches whenever the chance arose. He treated her like she was important. Precious, even.

He didn't just open up a new world for her — Atticus made her believe that she had her own special place in it.

That was why it was so hard whenever the spell broke. He'd given her a taste of more than just his blood, and every minute she went without it hurt just a bit more than the last.

But she didn't want to think about that. Not when they sat in a small, two person booth in the far corner of the bar area after hours of laughter. She was breathless and a thin layer of sweat slicked her spine as she wiggled onto the sparkly vinyl seat. Atticus sprawled beside her, his knee touching hers, and shot her a goofy, lopsided grin.

"Having fun, doll?"

"So much," she answered, slouching over onto her folded arms. The glowing, rubbery bracelets would leave dents in her cheek, but she didn't care.

Atticus's smile softened. "Good. I want you to try all the fun shit you never got to do. I remember how it felt to do stuff like this for the first time with the boss. My parents never would have cared enough to take us to an arcade or anything. It meant the world to me." He nudged her beneath the table. "It feels nice being able to do it for someone else."

A bucket of ice water couldn't have doused her hazy golden glow any more effectively. Carmine's throat went tight. For a glorious couple hours she'd let herself forget, but that time had passed.

This isn't a date. He's not mine. This is... Her first thought was *charity,* but that wasn't right either. It was some messed up cross between that and a friendly responsibility.

Feeling both ungrateful and foolish, Carmine pushed through the muck of her feelings to ask a question that had sat heavily on her heart. "What happened to your parents?"

"Died in a fire," he answered, fiddling with the label on his bottle. "About a month after I stupidly tried pickpocketing the UTA's most dangerous assassin, our piece of shit apartment building caught on fire." His throat bobbed with a hard swallow when he gestured to it. "That's why I sound like this. Smoke inhalation fucked up my throat."

The hair on her arms stood on end. She assumed they weren't around anymore for one reason or another, but that was worse than she could have imagined. She'd seen victims of fires on her slab. She *knew* the damage and the pain something as innocuous as smoke, let alone fire, could cause. "You were *inside?*"

"Not for the start, no. I was running errands for the boss in exchange for synth money when I saw the smoke coming from our block. I ran back because Adriana was in there. Probably wouldn't have bothered otherwise."

"Why?"

"Because they weren't good people, doll. They'd started to talk about my sister." A stark, dangerous look crossed his face. "She was barely more than a toddler and they were *hoping* she was neutral so they could sell her off. I'd planned on running away with her, which is part of why I needed the money from the boss, but the fire saved me the trouble."

A lot of things about Atticus made sense to her then. *No wonder he's so protective of me.*

It wasn't about her, but about what had shaped him. Atticus had been protecting his people since he was a child himself. He'd jumped at the chance to save her because that was what he'd always done, and now he was stuck with her like a stray he fed one too many times.

A strange mix of guilt and pride for the man he'd managed to become twisted her up. Carmine's voice came out as a croak when she asked, "You got hurt when you rescued Adriana. Was it bad?"

"Nasty smoke inhalation, some small burns. Nothing too bad." He waved a hand as if to bat away the memory. "I showed up on the boss's steps covered in ash, holding my baby sister, and passed out pretty much as soon as he cracked the door open. Then we just... never left."

Merciful One bless Harlan Bounds.

She'd seen the devotion in the eyes of his men, the love that radiated from his anchor and daughter, but now she *got* it. He was a hard, dangerous man, but he'd earned every ounce of loyalty he was given.

She was grateful for what had been done for her, but she *loved* Harlan Bounds for what he'd done for her anchor.

"I'm glad," she whispered, holding onto her biceps to keep from reaching for the vampire across the table. "I'm not glad you had bad parents, but I'm glad you found a good one. Now you can live whatever kind of life you want."

Atticus leaned forward, nearly mimicking her pose, and replied, "You can, too, you know?"

"I do know."

It's now or never, Carmine. You can't keep yearning for something he doesn't want to give you.

Trying to summon a well of optimism she didn't feel, Carmine informed him, "I think in a few months, when I'm settled at the funeral home, I'll look at getting a place in Pineridge."

Between one blink and the next, Atticus's expression blanked. "What are you talking about?"

Too filled with nervous energy to remain slouched, Carmine sat back, adjusted her bracelets, and then placed her sweaty palms in her lap. "I know you feel obligated to look after me, but I really can't— You've given me everything I need to figure my life out, Atticus. It's not right for me to keep leaning on you and everyone else. And—"

Carmine stopped herself. Forced air into her lungs. Tried to stop the screaming in her mind.

She couldn't bear to go *far,* not when she'd just found the closest thing to a family she'd had since she was six, but the more she considered the issue, the more resolute she became.

I can't cling to him.

He'd let her. He'd never push her away or tell her to stand on her own two feet, no matter how much money was in her new bank account or how it might stunt his own life. He'd accept her.

But in that moment Carmine understood something crucial: *She* couldn't accept that. She couldn't take advantage of his kindness, and she couldn't exist in a perpetual agony of desire, either. If there was a chance for them to be equals, *friends,* then she had to figure out how to survive on her own. Mostly, anyway.

There wasn't a chance she'd stop helping Zia in the greenhouse or pushing Serafina on the swing set, let alone cut out Adri-ana, the only person who'd ever truly *understand*.

She had to force the next words out past a wave of nausea. "You'll go through some withdrawal, so it would be best if I stop feeding from you soon."

Nerves jangling, Carmine peered at him, trying to gauge his expression, but he might as well have been carved from stone. Not knowing what else to do, she continued, "I'm so grateful for everything you've done for me, but I hate feeling like you— like you need to look after me all the time, that you have to let me feed. It's not right. An anchor should— I can't ask you to be that when you don't feel the same as I do."

It nearly killed her to gesture around them, to the atmosphere that had brought her so much joy just moments prior. "I love that you want to share these things with me, but I'm not a kid sister you need to babysit, or some helpless victim you're stuck with now. It's okay. I can manage just fine on my own. You should live your life without being tied down to some weird temple girl you found in the back of a trailer."

"What the *fuck?*"

Her gaze, which had wandered to the bar sometime during her ramble, snapped back to Atticus. She blanched.

He wasn't blank anymore. He looked *furious*.

Pressing his palms flat against the tabletop, he slowly leaned over it until he was mere inches from her face. Speaking in a soft, deadly voice, he asked, "Is that how you think I see you? As some sort of stray I'm stuck with?"

If she could have sucked the words from the air, she would have. Carmine's cheeks got hot when she amended, "Well, no, I think we're friends, but..."

"But what?"

"But... But I think you feel obligated to take care of people, and I don't want that to be the only reason you... you know, with me."

It was a bitter irony that she now understood how he must

have felt the first time she fed from him. The idea that he might only be *enduring* their intimate moments when they were what she lived for was too painful to bear.

It wasn't just physical. It wasn't just biology. It was connection. Intimacy. Something she only ever wanted to share with him, and memories she'd cherish for the rest of her life.

But if they meant little to him, if he only touched her and let her feed because he felt he *had* to... All of it would be tainted.

Her muscles bunched as fight or flight instincts screamed. Humiliation was a million mean little bugs crawling all over her skin. She wished they were real and that they'd pick the flesh from her bones already. Anything was better than hearing the dull *thunk* of his bottle hitting the table top, or the way he grabbed her hand and began to drag her out of the arcade.

Carmine stumbled after him, still a little clumsy in her new tennis shoes. The flashing lights of the arcade were a blur to her watery eyes. That was probably why it took her a while to realize they weren't headed for the door.

Atticus took a sharp right and dragged her down a hallway she'd seen people loitering around all night. Without saying a word, he pulled her into a room full of— *pods?*

She blinked, totally lost, as he angrily poked at a screen on the outside of the nearest one. The door to the pod opened with a musical chime, revealing another big screen and a bench. She barely had time to read the glowing words *"photo booth"* above the door before she'd been dragged inside.

It was outrageously bright inside, but that was only an issue for her sensitive eyes for a moment, because no sooner had the door closed than Atticus was pressing her against it, his big body blocking out everything else.

Rough hands cupped her cheeks and tilted her head back. He kicked the inside of her foot, spreading her legs, and filled the gap with one of his thighs. In what felt like a second, everything she saw, felt, and breathed was *him*.

"Atticus, what—"

"It was Atty earlier," he rumbled, expression cut so fierce it made a shock of something potent run down her spine. Fear, maybe, but also an arousal so deep and base, it came from some distant animal relative. "I want you to call me Atty. Loved ones call me Atty."

Loved ones?

"Okay," she wheezed, not following his train of thought. That didn't seem important compared to what they'd just been talking about.

"And I want you to know something else."

"What?"

His thumbs curved over her cheekbones as he dipped his head, bringing them so close that their breath mingled. "Not for one fucking second has this been about *babysitting* you. You think I would let just anyone bite me? You think I'd be out of my mind for a woman I felt *obligated* to take care of? You think I'd count down the minutes until I can lick your pussy again every fucking day if I didn't want you? All of you?"

Carmine's eyes went wide. "But you haven't said anything. You— you don't feed from me. You've never made any claim." And Atticus was nothing if not direct. If he wanted her as badly as she wanted him, wouldn't he have at least *hinted* that was the case?

A look of intense incredulousness crossed his face. "Doll, did you really not realize we've been dating this whole time?"

"Atty," she squeaked, "how am I supposed to know we're *dating* if I've never done it before? I was told to expect that when a man wants me, he'll take me. Feed from me. Claim me so no one else does. You... haven't."

He made the funniest garbled sound before choking out, "I thought you knew. I was waiting for you to tell me when you were ready, so *you* didn't feel obligated." Pain tightened the skin around his eyes. "Is that why you've been pulling away from me? I thought you'd changed your mind. I thought maybe you didn't want me anymore, that maybe now that you were getting your feet under you, you'd decided you didn't—"

"*Want* you?" She sucked in an incredulous breath. "I can't breathe when we're apart, and I need your smiles, and I can't drink any more synth, and I never even wanted a bite before, but when I think about *you*— Atty, I never even let myself dream of feeling an ounce of the happiness I feel when I'm with—"

The kiss was jarring, bone-rattling, all fang and tongue and the press of his hard body into hers. Atticus kissed her like he wanted to devour her, and Carmine kissed him like she wanted to be devoured. Her confession died in her throat. Whatever words she might have spoken were pressed into his lips and tangled around his seeking tongue.

I love you, she told him. *I want you. You're mine. Let me be yours.*

CHAPTER EIGHTEEN

ATTICUS HAD BEEN GOOD. HE'D WAITED. HE'D BEEN patient, even when it felt like he was being eaten alive by desire.

Carmine needed time, and watching her slowly come into her own on the estate was a thing of beauty. He loved watching her discover herself. The sound of her laughter, the easy way she fit in with his family, the profound joy she took in the simplest things — it all carried him through the unbearable hours he spent waiting for her to give him the sign that she was ready for him.

He knew that he was greedy, and maybe saying he had been patient was a bit of a stretch when he monopolized her time and touched her every chance he got, but for a vampire that had chosen his anchor, he thought he'd done pretty fucking well.

Whenever he had a spare moment, he tried to think of new things for her to experience — a state fair, a two-night river cruise, dancing in a renovated fire station-turned-club, trips to bookshops and museums — and he treasured every smile, gasp, and question she aimed his way. Even when they did nothing more than sit on the couch and watch movies, her legs slung over his lap and his arm stretched across the cushions to play with her hair, he was more fulfilled than he had been in his entire life.

It turned out that he hadn't been missing the excitement of crime. He'd been missing a *purpose.*

That purpose was experiencing life through Carmine's curious eyes, watching that shy smile unfurl, tasting her hot little cunt, and feeling her sharp little fangs sliding into his throat. Every feeding, every touch, every night that crawled by without claiming her made him more certain that she was it for him.

And she tried to *leave.*

A flush of panic prickled his skin even as he pressed his lips against hers in a desperate, hungry kiss. The idea that he might think of her as anything less than his perfect anchor was so outrageous that he struggled to process it.

But what was she supposed to think when I never said the words?

Atticus assumed she'd just *know.* She would understand why he offered his blood at every opportunity, why he took her out every chance he got, why he couldn't quite stop himself from touching her even when he tried so hard to give her space. He was giving her room to grow and come to him in her own time. He was building trust and making damn sure that she didn't feel like she *had* to reciprocate his feelings.

But he'd over-corrected. Carmine didn't have any references to hold him up to, only the harsh, black and white bullshit the crypt had beaten into her about what to expect from a relationship. Was it any wonder that she'd misread his attempts to court her?

"I'm obsessed with you," he breathed against her swollen lips. "You're the first thing I think about when I wake up and the last thing I think about before I go to sleep. I dream about how you taste and I— Fuck, doll, I'd do anything to make you mine."

A saccharine jingle from the photobooth's console might have ruined the moment if Carmine hadn't slipped her soft hands under the hem of his t-shirt to stroke his skin. He hissed, his abdominal muscles tensing even as his venom gland pulsed angrily, desperate for relief. The pain from it had become nearly unbearable over the last several weeks, but he'd endured it. She was worth any pain, any sacrifice.

"Why didn't you say so?"

"I had to give you time," he rasped, dipping his head to press a hot, open-mouthed kiss to her neck. Her breath hitched and his cock, painfully hard behind his fly, jerked. He'd damn near rubbed it raw over the past several weeks, but not even a bit of chafing would stop it from finally, finally having her. "Couldn't rush you. Couldn't violate your trust. Had to make sure you knew—"

"That you're mine?"

He could only groan. Speech was beyond him as he mindlessly mouthed at her neck, the instinct to bite screaming inside him.

Carmine's curious fingers dipped to the button of his jeans. "When we were stopped at that checkpoint and Captain Bennet asked me if I wanted to get away from you, I told them that you were mine."

The console squealed with tinny, upbeat music as a cheerful androgynous voice ran through the instructions on how to take their pictures, but none of that made an impression on him as he gasped, "You did?"

"I hoped," she whispered, popping the brass button through the loop. The zipper went next, the teeth coming apart slowly as she dragged the tab down. "I wanted it to be true."

He knew he should stop her. They were in a public place — one with a camera, no less — and the instinct to get her somewhere dark and secluded pounded him from all sides, but very little had changed since her first feeding in the RV.

He was still weak, reduced to nothing but base urges and pleasure when she caressed the flat of his stomach and crisp line of hair that disappeared into his briefs. Atticus was helpless. He'd give her anything, everything, no matter where or when she asked for it.

And when she looked up at him like that, when she whispered her desires against his lips...

"I never wanted to be someone's blood bride, but when I'm with you, I don't feel like one. I feel like I'm home."

He was a goner.

Atticus was forced to slap his palms against the photobooth's door when her fingers slid under the waistband of his underwear to brush against his tortured cock. He hunched his shoulders, blocking her from whatever view the camera might've had, and croaked, "You're not a blood bride to me. You're my whole world."

A hiss of relief escaped from between his teeth when she freed him from the wretched confines of his briefs. Carmine touched him experimentally, her expression intensely focused as she adjusted to the weight of him in her hand. She wore that look again, the one that turned him on like nothing else: the look that said he was her plaything, her experiment, and all he had to do was sit back and take whatever she chose to give him.

"You don't want me to give you heirs."

It wasn't a question, but he answered her anyway. "Not anytime soon, and not unless *you* want kids. And just so you know, I got the birth control shot years ago. I can't get you pregnant until I get that reversed." Birth control wasn't something most vampires thought about, what with their intense breeding drive and the long process of preparing an anchor for the endeavor, but he wasn't a man who took chances.

She rewarded him with a slow stroke. "You don't care about prestige."

"I don't give a fuck about prestige." He spread his legs a little, trying to keep his balance as his knees threatened to give out on him. "Fuck, doll, you're killing me."

Carmine glanced up at him with wide blue eyes. "Am I doing it wrong? I studied—"

He couldn't stop the low, garbled sound that escaped his throat. "You're perfect. I just don't want our first time to be in a fuckin' photo booth, and I've been waiting for this for so long that I might not make it even that far if you keep this up."

"Oh." Her gaze darted down to where she held his cock in her silken fist. The strobing lights from the photo booth, hot pink and blue, caught in the beads of pre-come that crowned the head. "*Oh.*"

Atticus tried to catch his breath, but it was pointless when she took it away again just as quickly. "Take me home, then," she demanded, arching onto the balls of her feet to nibble on his lower lip. Those perfect fangs pricked his lip, making them both groan.

It killed him to say it, but Atticus had to ask, "Are you sure? We don't have to rush. I'll go as slow as you need me to, doll."

His hips jerked when she gave him a firm squeeze. "You told me sex is sacred when it's with the right person, the right chemistry, the right time."

Claws digging into the wall, he hissed, "I did."

"You're the right person." She stroked him, slow and tight. "This is the right chemistry." Her fangs pressed into his lip again, drawing the smallest amount of blood. She lapped it up as she stroked his cock. His brain short-circuited. "This is the right time, Atty. I know it."

"*Fuck.*"

He had to stop her or he really would come all over her hand. It was hot as fuck that she didn't care that they were still sort of in public, but his instincts were going haywire, demanding he throw her over his shoulder and hide her away someplace where no one else could see, hear, or smell her. He was desperate to satisfy Carmine, but the instinct to claim was walloped by the compulsion to protect her.

Panting, he dropped his hands to crush her to his chest, effectively pinning her arm between them so she was forced to stop her erotic torture. "Okay. Okay. We're going home. Now."

"Wait."

His heart dropped into his stomach. "What? What's wrong?"

Carmine tilted her head back to give him a slow, mischievous smile. "Can we take a picture first?"

CHAPTER NINETEEN

ALL TOLD, CARMINE HAD SPENT A LOT OF TIME watching Atticus drive. The way he held himself, the motions of the vehicle, the speed at which he drove — she thought she had all those things well-categorized and filed in her mind.

She'd *never* seen him drive like he did that night.

Carmine gripped the arm rests of her seat and laughed with exhilaration as he hurtled up the mountain roads. There was no fear, no worry that they'd career over the edge and plummet into the frigid river below. Her trust in Atticus was bone-deep. He wouldn't let anything happen to her. Not now. Not ever.

They made it back to the estate in record time.

Anticipation was a warm, heavy weight in her stomach. Her pulse beat between her thighs. Her panties were wet. Longing unlike any she'd known gripped her as she recalled the weight of him in her palm, the scent of his skin, and his harsh gasps in her ear.

Atticus had been too focused on navigating the tight, winding roads of the mountains to touch her as they drove, but once they made it onto the estate, his palm landed on her thigh, so close to the gusset of her jeans that his pinkie brushed the seam.

Before she could so much as gasp, he'd moved to cup her

instead, pressing so firmly that her hips lifted reflexively off the seat.

"I think about this pussy every fuckin' night," he growled, turning the car onto the private road that led to the cottages. "I love how wet you get when you feed from me, and I lose my mind when you come. It's the most beautiful thing in the world."

He pressed his two middle fingers into the seam, applying pressure where she needed it most. "Atty," she breathed, grasping his tattooed forearm like a lifeline.

"It's going to be even more beautiful seeing you wrapped around my cock." He glanced at her, his jaw flexing. "You ready for that?"

"Gods, yes." She didn't hesitate, didn't consider the repercussions or the fear that had always clouded her imaginings of intercourse. What had once seemed like a harsh inevitability had revealed itself to be a source of joy and anticipation.

Atticus had introduced her to sex with care. He'd wrung orgasm after orgasm out of her without once asking for anything in return. He let her lead, and his touch was rarely uncomfortable and never unwanted. Carmine couldn't imagine that penetrative sex would be any different — except, perhaps, in that it would be *better*.

He flashed a fanged smile full of promise. "Good."

The tires squealed as he came to an abrupt stop in front of his cottage. All of the homes on the estate looked similar, each one assembled with discarded stone from the mine, old bricks, and local timber. Inside, however, each one had been renovated to suit the owner's taste. Carmine was intimately familiar with Atticus's dark wood accents, clean lines, and white walls. His taste ran more Spartan than her own, but it suited him. It also pleased the part of her that desired order and cleanliness both in the morgue and in her living space.

She wasn't thinking of any of that, though, as Atticus yanked her door open and practically dragged her out of the car. She laughed and scrambled to keep up with him as he pulled her toward the cottage.

For all that they were in a rush, they couldn't seem to stop themselves from pausing every few steps to allow their greedy hands to wander, grab, stroke, and pull. Their kisses were hungry and increasingly desperate. Atticus's taste always drove her wild, but her desire was sharpened to a keen edge by this new hunger he revealed.

Her back hit the heavy wooden door with a *thump*. Atticus cupped the side of her neck with one hand, his thumb tilting her chin up, as his other fumbled with the biometric lock. Their mouths were fused, their kisses raw and wet. Her hands roamed beneath the stretchy material of his shirt, tracing all the flesh that had been barred to her for too long.

She tore her mouth away from his to pant, "I want to see you. You've never let me see you before."

"Couldn't risk it." The lock beeped. Atticus pushed the door open and walked her inside. He licked at her lips, lapping like he couldn't get enough of her taste, even as he kicked the door shut behind them. "Thought if I got naked I'd lose any sense I had left."

"I want you to lose your sense," she replied, tugging at his shirt. "I never thought I'd have someone who wanted me so much that they'd lose their head. I never thought it'd be this good."

Being a blood bride meant being possessed, used, even coveted. It wasn't the same as being desired — not just as a vessel, but as *her*. Carmine Safi. A woman who liked sparkly eyeshadow, arcades, murder mystery shows, and Atticus Caldwell.

He huffed a dry, incredulous laugh against her lips. "Gods, Carmine, I haven't had my head on straight since I opened that fuckin' trailer. I'm crazy about you. Love how stubborn you are, how smart. I love how you smell and how you taste and when you look at me like I'm a science experiment. I hate when we're apart and I count the minutes until I see you again."

"Me, too." She didn't bother looking behind her as he walked her backward toward his underground bedroom. He wouldn't let her bump into anything. "I thought it might dim a little when things settled down, but..."

But it hadn't. It'd only simmered in the back of her mind, getting warmer, sweeter, more complex. While she'd adjusted to life outside the crypt and actually got to know him, her desire had quietly permeated every cell of her body, changing her fundamentally.

"It didn't," he finished for her, gritty and knowing. "It only got stronger."

She dragged her blunt claws down his chest. *"Yes."*

Atticus hissed. Without warning, she was hoisted up into his arms. Her legs banded around his waist as he supported her weight with a forearm under her backside.

"Duck your head," he growled.

Carmine didn't need to be told twice. She pressed her kiss-swollen lips to his throat, tasting the delicious, familiar tang of his skin as he jogged down the short flight of stairs to his bedroom.

He told her that it had once been a root cellar, but she wasn't exactly certain what the purpose of one was. It had something to do with food, she was fairly sure, which explained why he'd converted it into a bedroom. Not only was it light-proof, but it was below ground — something that called to a vampire's instincts and made her feel safe.

Most vampires didn't really need to live underground anymore, as many made do with light-proofing technology, canopied beds, and other methods of achieving the confined feeling they craved, but Carmine had lived most of her life underground, so she appreciated it immensely.

Like the rest of his house, his bedroom was sparsely decorated and tidy. His bed took up the vast majority of the room. It was soft, and when he lowered her onto it, a cloud of his scent enveloped her.

Carmine wiggled beneath him, too eager to shuck her own clothes to be anything near dignified. He helped her strip with an equal amount of enthusiasm. When he pulled her jeans off, he did so with enough force to nearly yank her off the bed. They both exploded into laughter as she clawed at the duvet.

"Sorry." He shook his head and gave her a wry grin. "I should go slower. I want your first time to be—"

"With you, right here, right now." She tossed her bra onto the floor and reached for the band of her panties, her hips lifting. "I don't care if it's fast. I don't care if it's not perfect. I only care that it's *you.*"

Atticus planted a fist by her hip, his shoulders hunching as he closed his eyes. He breathed deeply through his nose before whispering, "Luckiest fuckin' man in the world."

Opening his eyes, he braced a knee on the bed and levered himself up. Atticus favored black clothing, which made his skin seem all the more pale. He pulled his shirt over his head, his torso stretching as he lifted his arms. She was transfixed by the sight of so much of that fair skin as it was revealed to her.

Atticus was not a man with superfluous muscle. He was dense, strong. The lines of his abdomen were sturdy, his shoulders broad, and his movements tightly controlled.

And the tattoos that decorated all that perfect, pale flesh were...

"Gorgeous," she breathed.

He was perfect. Perfectly real, solid, *him.* If she'd ever dared to dream of an anchor, she would have imagined someone like him.

Black ink stretched down from the neck tattoos she knew so well. They covered his chest and abdomen with all sorts of imagery. A lot of it was floral, but there were skulls, knives, and religious iconography she identified immediately. She'd once asked him if his tattoos had a meaning — something she'd always wondered and never got the chance to ask her dead friends from the slab — but he'd only shrugged.

"Nah," he'd explained. *"Only a few mean anything. Most of it I got because I liked it."*

He'd shown her the ones that did have meaning, though —

the paintbrush for his sister, the north star for Harlan, the roses for Zia, and the baby's handprint for Serafina. But he hadn't shown her everything, and he certainly hadn't revealed the inflamed, fresh-looking tattoo on his left pec.

Carmine blinked. Sitting up abruptly, she hooked her fingers into the belt loops of his pants, pulling him closer. She gaped at her name, inked in what she recognized as his own handwriting, over his heart.

Atticus went very still as he let her look her fill. When she could finally tear her eyes away from it long enough to glance at him, he offered a lopsided smile. "Whatever happens with us, my heart's yours. I'm yours."

"You're mine," she breathed, just to feel the words on her lips again. She wanted them carved into her marrow, into her flesh and soul just as surely it had been inked into his.

Cupping her jaw with both hands, he pressed a heart-stopping kiss to her lips. "I'm yours."

"I want to be yours, too." Carmine gripped his hips with greedy fingers. "Bite me."

"Not until I'm inside you." But even as he said it, Atticus's fangs scraped her lip and moved down, leaving stinging trails over her jaw and the line of her throat.

Carmine's heart pounded. Her fingers shook, too, but they still managed to find the button and fly of his jeans. Pushing them and his briefs down his strong thighs, she immediately sought out the hot bar of his cock.

Giving it a slow stroke, she gasped, "Then I need you inside me. Now."

She wasn't entirely sure what happened, but in the next moment she was spun around, her cheek pressed into the blankets, and her backside in the air. Atticus kept one firm hand on the back of her neck while the other trailed over her flank and between her legs to spread her thighs.

"Can't look in those eyes," he rumbled, his voice gritty with want, "or this will be over before it starts."

Carmine slapped one hand on the bed in protest. Her own growl built in her throat. "Atty—"

"Shh, I've got you. I've always got you." Featherlight and torturous, he trailed the pads of his fingers over her slick cunt, parting her, until he found what he was looking for. Her hips jerked when he circled her clitoris, lightly at first and then with increasing pressure.

She clenched, hips rolling. They'd done this part many times. Atticus had become something of an expert at how to make her orgasm, and she feared that was exactly why he wasn't employing any of his usual tricks. Instead, he brought her to the brink, only to pull back a moment before she went over the edge.

His fingers moved away just in time, a mere moment before the first sparks of her orgasm began to flicker. A whine replaced her growl.

Warmth seeped into her back as he leaned over her, covering her with his wider body. His lips skimmed her shoulder, teasing her with the tips of his fangs and the hot, wet glide of his tongue.

"My beautiful little doll," he murmured, the gentle tone giving her no warning before he thrust two fingers inside her.

Carmine's back arched, her muscles spasming around his fingers, but she couldn't move far when he pressed his greater weight down on her. A garbled, helpless sound escaped her throat when began to shuttle his fingers in and out with obscene, sticky sounds. The gentleness was gone. Now his touch was urgent, almost too much.

In between peppering kisses across her shoulder and the nape of her neck, he gravely assured her, "You can take this, doll. Fuck yourself back on my hand. *Fuck.* Yes, just like that. Such a perfect, perfect little doll."

The matron had always warned that sex would most likely be unpleasant at best, but Atticus had gone to great pains to show her that wasn't the case. With him, even the overwhelming, borderline painful parts of sex were pleasurable. She often stayed up well past dawn, her thoughts consumed by the sting between her legs, the bruising of her nipples that had been loved almost too much, and the soreness of her muscles after he bent her into some improbable shape.

So when he slid another finger in, stretching her past the point of fullness as he whispered praise in her ear, and kept up that relentless pace, Carmine didn't balk or panic. She submitted to the sensations, the sparks of pleasure and the burn of the intrusion, and clung to the smoky sound of his voice guiding her to the precipice.

She rocked her hips back, desperately meeting his pistoning fingers. Familiar wet sounds filled the air. Carmine lurched toward her orgasm, pushed a little further each time he dragged his fingertips over the sensitive spot inside her. It was a brutal thing that awaited her, an orgasm unlike any he'd given her before — a shattering force that shortened her breath and threatened to remake her, cell by cell.

A scream erupted from her throat when he yanked his hand back. Her hips moved uselessly, undulating beneath him in a fruitless attempt to regain their fullness. Instinct howled at his cruelty, at his lack of claim.

The animal part of her wanted to tear at him for abandoning her right when she needed him most, when she was nearly claimed and bred. Higher thought had already shut down. There was no reasoning, no logic, no quiet voice reminding her that instinct wasn't reality and there would be no real breeding this time.

There was only the wildfire of her need and the feral urge that compelled her to scream and hiss and claw at him until he claimed her in all ways.

Atticus sat up, leaving her sweat-slicked flesh cold. Before she could demand his return, she was flipped onto her back again.

Carmine stared up at him through watery eyes, her chest heaving, and dug her fingers into the sheets. *"Please,"* she begged, spreading her thighs as wide as they could go. "Please, Atty. *Please."*

His cheeks were flushed, the look in his eyes wild. The shock of ginger hair on his head was mussed, and when she glanced down, she found his cock lined up with her cunt, ruddy, veined, and quite a bit larger than his fingers.

The blunt tip pressed in. "Keep your eyes on me," he grated. "I want to see them when I make you come on my cock."

It was hard to do as he commanded when the sting of his entry made her eyes water even more than they already were, but Carmine did her best. Even if he hadn't ordered her to, she would have. The sight of him slowly pushing into her body, the striking lines of his face, the way his eyes blazed with the same wildness she felt...

She wouldn't have missed that for anything.

His rough palms landed on her inner thighs, pushing them as far as they could go before he gripped them hard. "Deep breath, doll."

Carmine sucked in a lungful of air heavy with their scents, but it exploded out of her not a moment later when he sheathed himself in one forceful thrust.

Her back arched off the bed. "Atty!"

Letting go of her trembling thighs, Atticus braced his palms by her ears and bent over her. Their noses brushed as their harsh breaths mingled. "You okay, doll?" he gasped, cupping the crown of her head.

Carmine fought to catch her breath, to think around the burn and stretch of what felt like an invasion. Her body didn't feel like her own anymore. It was a different thing, all of her nerves misfiring, sending conflicting information to her brain.

She wasn't sure she liked having his cock inside her. It was too much. Too full. He'd impaled her, pinned her there beneath his bulk, and while her instincts crowed with victory, her mind hadn't yet caught up to why that was a good thing. Understanding the mechanics of the body had always grounded her, but in this instance she thought perhaps every textbook, every observation she'd made on the slab, was wrong.

This can't be right. He 's not supposed to fit in there.

Desperate to make some sense of things, Carmine wrapped her arms around him. Feeling the sweaty topography of his muscles, she whimpered, "I need you."

"You have me." He sipped at her lips with small, reverent kisses. "You have all of me, Carmine. I'll make this better. Just relax. Breathe for me."

Her lashes were heavy with tears, but she nodded. "Okay."

Still sheathed to the hilt, he gently turned her head to one side, presenting her throat to his questing mouth.

Her breath caught. All thoughts of burning muscles and size incompatibility were shunted aside.

Yes, she thought, toes curling. *Finally.*

She craved his bite, his claim. It was exactly what she needed to find her pleasure again.

Atticus whispered something against her skin, the softest *I love you,* before his fangs slid through. There was the smallest flash of pain, barely anything compared to the burn between her legs, and then... *euphoria.*

Warmth spread from that perfect bite. It bled into her veins like the sweetest syrup. Every beat of her heart spread it a little further, until she could taste it in the thin lining of her cheeks and feel it all the way down in her toes.

Her muscles loosened. The discomfort faded. Her world went hazy and bright while her mind went blissfully quiet. There was nothing but slow-burning pleasure and contentment in her when his fangs slid free and he began to suck, taking small, greedy gulps of her blood.

One of his hands framed the side of her face. She turned her head a bit more, seeking out his thumb. Carmine pressed a kiss to the pad. In response, he slipped it past her lips and pressed down on her tongue, silently commanding her to suck. His low, pleased rumble vibrated through her chest when she hollowed her cheeks around it.

Atticus's hips began to move. He didn't thrust, but swiveled his hips, reigniting nerves. She clutched at his back and lifted her hips, intoxicated by the burgeoning pleasure and the venom coursing through her veins.

He's mine, she thought, tasting the salt of his skin with deep, dark pleasure. *I'm his.*

The crypt taught her that she would only ever belong *to* someone, never that someone could belong to her, too. It was the height of decadence to know that a man such as Atticus Caldwell was hers and hers alone.

She didn't mean to bite his thumb. It was pure instinct to sink the tip of a fang into his flesh, drawing just enough blood to make her moan.

His rhythm stuttered. The suction on her throat ended and was replaced by the flat of his tongue. "Perfect," he breathed, thrusting harder, a little deeper. Pleasure sparked whenever he hit that spot inside her as he slid out and once again when he thrust home. "So fuckin' perfect."

One hand grabbed her thigh and pressed it upward, into his chest, as he bent to lower his lips to her breasts. She lapped at the tiny wound she'd made on his thumb even as he pricked the sensitive skin of her nipple with his fangs. Pleasure, sharper than any she'd felt before, snapped down her spine.

She was nearly mindless with it as he bit, sucked, and thrust inside her, his speed increasing until her own hips could no longer keep up. Their bodies met with obscene sounds, wet ones and slapping ones and beautiful, breathy groans neither could contain. Atticus slid his thumb free from her lips just as he began to pound into her, each thrust so brutal it threatened to hike her up the bed.

Holding her there with one arm bracketed above her head, he stooped to give her a raw, bloody kiss. His other hand snuck between them. She shouted something — his name, a declaration, a curse, who knew — when he rolled her clitoris between his thumb and forefinger.

Her orgasm, built up and pushed down so many times, whited out her vision. Carmine's muscles seized. The taste of their blood mingling on her tongue sent her higher, and his frantic thrusts, graceless and desperate, were followed by a warm gush somewhere deep inside.

Vampiric instincts were like static in the background of her mind, a constant low-level hum of perfect contentment now that they had what they wanted: a mate, the chance to breed, and blood so sweet, it was all she'd crave for the rest of her life.

Pressing her forehead to his, Carmine whispered, "I couldn't have dreamed of this."

Their bodies were still joined, their skin slippery with sweat, but neither cared when Atticus gathered her close and squeezed her like she was the most precious thing in the world.

"Neither could I," he replied, hoarse with feeling. "When I opened that trailer, I never... It never occurred to me that I'd find my everything inside."

Carmine smiled, slow and achingly tender. "I'm still not sorry I ran."

His huff of laughter puffed against her cheeks. "No?"

"No, because you caught me."

"I'll always catch you," he promised.

She stroked her fingers through his sweaty hair and, just because she wanted to hear him say it, she asked, "Why is that?"

Atticus pressed a reverent kiss to the fresh bite on her throat. "Because you're mine."

EPILOGUE

An excerpt from the article "Synthblood Manufacturer Sold: UniSynth Saved by Local Businessman" written by Nasir Patton for *The Sacramento Hive*, dated February 30th, 2049—

After the untimely death of its owner, local synthblood brand UniSynth was destined for bankruptcy. Hubert Todd Junger, a vampire and businessman who passed away in his home in May, left his company in a bind.

During his life, whispers and accusations plagued his leadership, and after his death, many in the company openly speculated that he'd been siphoning money from UniSynth for years, funding a lavish lifestyle. Some evidence of this has since come to light, and many of the high ranking members of the company have abandoned ship, leaving behind a mound of debt and over a hundred distressed, mostly vampiric, employees.

One of the rare synthblood manufacturers on the West Coast, the company that had been flourishing, despite what now appears to be criminally bad leadership. This would have been a blow not just to the local economy, but to the small but growing vampire community in the Sierras.

Synthblood is costly to produce and store, making importation across territory lines a hassle. With most manufacturers located across the continent in the Neutral Zone — and the prices of their product correspondingly high — losing a local company means that vampires will have even fewer cost-effective options for something that is necessary for their very survival.

Understandably, the speculation around Junger's death and its effect on UniSynth was the cause of a lot of anxiety amongst Sacramento's vampires. Notable among them was local businessman Harlan Bounds, owner of Empire LLC and Empire Estate.

A quiet, reserved man, he's known for investing in several successful restaurants, start-ups, and charitable initiatives in small towns like Pineridge, Auburn, and Grass Valley.

Bounds purchased UniSynth with little fanfare. An announcement went out to employees Monday evening at nine PM introducing him as the new owner and outlining his vision for the future of the company:

We don't just make synth. We serve our community. Going forward, half of UniSynth's profits — a direct result of your labor — will go to charitable organizations that support causes like vampire health, outreach, and the safety of those of us who are venom neutral.

I ask that you help us in this mission, so we can all benefit from a stronger, more interconnected community. Let's do some good.

When asked what inspired the decision to turn a profitable company into a charitable one, Bounds answered simply, "I'm inspired by my family. They deserve a better world."

∽

"I think we should call it something fun," Zia suggested. She bounced Serafina on her knee, one hand on her daughter's soft belly and the other holding a steaming cup of cocoa to her lips. Serafina was getting just a little too big for her mother to easily bounce her, but she didn't seem to care as she played with her soft dragon plushie on the tabletop. She'd received it as a gift from her friend Emilia, a little dragon girl who lived in Pineridge, and it was an official member of the Empire family.

Almost every member of that family was crammed into the kitchen. The non-vampires picked over the abundance of baked goods Zia had whipped up for the meeting, while the vampires contented themselves with bottles of synth or nothing at all.

Harlan sat at the head of the table, one arm slung over the back of Zia's chair. His other hand was occupied with one of the many files scattered across the tabletop — tax records, expense reports, invoices, and every bit of the mess Junger had left his company when he got what he deserved.

Atticus sat beside his anchor, who was dressed in a sparkly top with her short, dark hair pulled back in a scrunchy and dangling, articulated skeleton earrings in her ears. They were pressed close together, their thighs touching beneath the table. Every time he shifted, he not only felt the warmth of her, but the pleasant ache of where she'd bitten him that dusk: right on the meat of his thigh, mere seconds after letting him come in that pretty doll's mouth of hers.

Gods, I love her.

When the news broke that Junger's business was going under, everyone except Carmine had scoffed and agreed it was his final punishment. He deserved no legacy, no remembrance. Every bit of him deserved to die, even if all that remained was a struggling synth brand. Atticus knew it bothered her, but he assumed it was the reminder of everything that'd happened to her that caused her upset. Knowing she liked to process things on her own for a while, he hadn't pushed her to talk to him until she was ready.

It shocked the shit out of him when, not two nights after the news of the company's possible bankruptcy broke, she asked if the money in her account was enough to buy UniSynth.

He wasn't sure, and more than that, he didn't understand why she'd want to save something that carried Junger's name in its legacy.

"Because," she'd answered, as frank and logical as she always was, *"he used the money from that company to do bad. Isn't it a better punishment to do the opposite? Grim says that we shouldn't meet acts of evil with evil, but with action. Besides, think of all the vampires who need that synth. I don't want anyone going hungry if I can help it."*

Even if he hadn't seen the wisdom in that, he still would have done whatever she asked of him. If Carmine wanted something, he found a way to get it for her, no questions asked.

Of course, it wasn't a simple operation. Buying up a floundering company wasn't something he had experience in, so he went to Harlan for advice. Of course that meant Zia, too. Soon enough, the entire estate was involved.

Carmine didn't want to be the face of the company, despite owning the majority stake by a slim margin, so it was decided that Harlan would step in. After much discussion and the rest of the men on the estate sticking their nose into stuff that wasn't their business, they decided to invest, too.

With the money lined up and Harlan's ability to intimidate even the gods used to their advantage, it didn't take long for the remaining members of UniSynth's board to sign over the company.

All the investors, save Adriana — who was busy with gods knew what in San Francisco — were gathered to decide on the company's new name.

Suggestions were thrown out from all corners of the kitchen, most of them ridiculous or exceedingly bad. Someone suggested Hot Blooded. Another threw out I Can't Believe It's Not Blood. When Tarrence, a shifter, had the bright idea to suggest Red Juice, Atticus slapped his hand on the table and ordered, "All right, everyone shut up! Your ideas are bad and you're not funny."

Michael, speaking from around a mouthful of steaming gözleme, muttered, "I thought Red Juice was pretty funny."

"You're not a vampire *and* you have a terrible sense of humor, so quiet." Turning to his anchor, who was making the face he recognized as her *I'm thinking* look, he asked in a much gentler tone, "What about you, doll? What do *you* want to name it?"

Carmine wasn't shy, but she still struggled to find her voice amongst the relative chaos of their friends and family. He'd gotten good at reading when she had something she wanted to say but couldn't find the space to get it out. When he spotted it, he always made a point to quiet everyone down, allowing her to speak in her own time.

No one ever complained or looked askance at her. The crew adored her, and the Bounds family loved her more. They could be a little too loud sometimes, but they tried hard to give her what she needed to flourish amongst them.

Part of it was out of love for Atticus, he knew, but that wasn't the main reason. Carmine just *fit*. She was the quiet, thoughtful friend Zia needed and the confidante Adriana never had. Her dry humor and blunt way of speaking delighted the guards. The director of the funeral home treated her like one of his grandkids, and the community of Pineridge breathed a sigh of relief, knowing she would likely take over for the old man when he retired.

Their lives fell into a comfortable groove, but there was no boredom, no dulling the spark that lit between them the night they met.

He'd never been as happy as he was when he simply basked in her. Atticus lived for every new discovery she made, every trip they took, every grin he received when he surprised her with a kiss. When they were together, everything was new and beautiful.

"I know what I want to name it," she said, big blue eyes moving as she made eye contact with everyone, including little

Serafina, who made her best attempt at a beastly growl and flapped her dragon's wings.

Settling his hand on her back, right where he could best feel her heartbeat, Atticus pressed, "Tell me."

She tipped her chin up and met his gaze. "New Life."

A hush settled over the room. It was a different kind of quiet than the one before it. His chest swelled with a potent mix of pride and tenderness as he gazed at his anchor. "For our new life?"

"Yes." Carmine looked around again. A small, soft smile pulled at her lips. "For all of our new lives."

He pressed his own smile into the crown of her head as murmurs of appreciation went around the kitchen.

New Life. New purpose. Everything I'll ever need.

Atticus silently counted the beats of her heart under his palm, treasuring each one, when he whispered, "I couldn't imagine anything better, doll."

THE END

A sneak peek of Devotion's Covenant...

May 2048 — San Francisco, The Elvish Protectorate

It was not the first time Petra Zaskodna sat across from a murderer. It would not be the last.

The bar wasn't filthy, not like many of the establishments she'd frequented since she was a little girl clinging to her father's coattails, but it had the patina of grime that came from something other than spilled beer and sweat. It was the sticky residue of the wretched.

No matter how well she played her role, Petra knew she would always find her kin in the wretched.

There was something comforting about being unseen amongst the dregs of the world. While she couldn't exactly say she missed it, Petra liked the honesty of the people who spent their time in bars like The Broken Tooth. Even when they lied, it was the honest sort: mumbled assurances that they had cut back on their drinking, outrage at being called out for cheating at poker, a cheerful assurance that they'd have the money soon, definitely, don't worry.

Everyone in the bar knew the secret language of those lies, so really, they weren't lies at all. Petra had learned that language early.

But in her new life, the stakes were a lot higher than a simple poker game in the back of a dive bar, or a dispute over a botched blood delivery between two upstart vampire families.

In her world, the lies she told would get her killed. Eventually.

Not tonight.

Tonight she relaxed in a dark corner booth Rasmus, the half-feral were who organized this meeting, had reserved for her. She pretended to nurse a glass of cheap red wine. A blues song buzzed through ancient speakers over her head and across the room. A cracked screen showed an endless loop of arena fights.

Petra canted her head to one side, scrutinizing the screen. The spray of cracks was definitely the result of a preternaturally strong fist. Or perhaps a head.

There hadn't been any fights yet, but she'd only been waiting for ten minutes. There was still plenty of time for one of the temperamental weres to start a brawl. The bar was their territory, but the other factions who called the underbelly of San Francisco home were always testing boundaries, jockeying for a better place in the hierarchy. That tension made the air endlessly combustible. Fights were inevitable and — mostly — harmless.

Her parents had lived that way. They died that way, too.

Petra ran her thumb over the thick stem of her wine glass, her gaze on the door. The bar wasn't particularly crowded and she wouldn't recognize the man she'd come to meet, but couldn't help but be on alert. Demons weren't common in the city, so she figured she'd be able to spot him.

But that wasn't the only reason she scanned the bar again and again. Even with her glamour in place, she worried someone would recognize her at any moment.

When she usurped the position of San Francisco's High Priestess, she didn't anticipate the level of notoriety it would come with. She hadn't thought that far ahead. Seeing as she so rarely ventured off of cathedral grounds, it wasn't normally an issue, but when she set up a meeting with one of the most dangerous men in the entire United Territories and Allies...

A knot of unease tightened in her belly. It'd been there ever since she stepped foot in the bar and had only gotten worse as she sat there, waiting for a monster to show his face.

Your glamour is perfect, she assured herself for the hundredth time. It was the one thing her arrant father, unable to use magic himself, had made sure she knew how to do.

"You can never have too many disguises," he'd told her with a pat to her head.

Petra had taken that bit of advice to heart. She'd welded it to her very soul, crafting armor layer by layer, mask by mask, until she knew she could survive anything — even a meeting with Shade.

Her glamour was more meticulously crafted than the average. Most were a simple smoke screen, a shifting, unfocused image of a face, but that in itself tended to attract attention in the same way a balaclava did. No, a much more effective but infinitely more magically difficult method was to create an illusion of a completely different face.

The woman sitting in the corner booth was not Petra Zaskodna, but a cute brunette with a snubbed nose, pale skin, and dark eyes. She wore Petra's clothes, but not her robes of office. No one would think to connect the esteemed High Priestess with a beaten leather jacket, slim-fitted jeans, and sturdy snakeskin boots.

And yet...

Petra licked her lips, tasting the ghost of wine there, and casually turned her head to take in the other side of the bar. The hair rose on the back of her neck.

She was being watched.

Considering she'd spent the last three years under near-constant, hidden surveillance, she knew the feeling well.

Her heart beat a quicker rhythm, but she was careful not to breathe too quickly or change her expression as she observed the patrons of the bar weaving around tables. She'd been busy watching the entrance, thinking that Shade would waltz in at any moment, so she hadn't done more than give the back of the bar a cursory look when she arrived.

Now she peered closer, into the smoky shadows that nearly obscured a beaten up pool table. A single light shaded by dusty stained glass hung over the table. Its glow barely penetrated the gloom in that far corner and, as she watched, it flickered, as if it struggled against the shadows.

It hadn't been that dark when she arrived.

She remembered seeing a few men gathered around, drunkenly arguing over what counted as hustling when she took her seat. The light was brighter then, and the glow of a branded neon sign had illuminated the far wall. At some point in the ten minutes she'd been there, it had been extinguished.

Petra's gaze flickered across the bar again, searching for vaguely familiar faces.

The men were gone. No one sat at the high tables closest to the pool table's dim alcove.

Petra's fingers curled reflexively around the stem of her wine glass. The knot of unease hardened into a stone, a heaviness in the pit of her stomach, as the sensation of being watched transitioned into the certainty that she was being hunted.

She knew that feeling well, too.

Carefully — oh-so-carefully — Petra turned her attention back to the alcove. It didn't matter how hard she strained to see into the shadows. She couldn't make out anything beyond the center of the pool table, lit with jaundiced light.

It flickered once. Twice.

It went out.

Fight or flight instincts surged. The sound of the drunken crowd, the tinny blues music, the clank of glasses on the tables —

all of it was muffled as every survival instinct strained to find the predator in the dark.

A pair of amber eyes flickered into being, twin flames struck into existence in the time between heartbeats. They peered back at her.

Petra didn't jump. Not exactly. Rather, she stiffened all at once, each muscle seizing until she was completely frozen there in the tacky booth, her fingers locked around her wine glass.

She couldn't look away. She knew those were eyes, but she struggled to accept it. In the darkness, they appeared to glow with an unnatural light — liquid metal heated to such a degree that they had their own luminescence. A light that was both beautiful and a warning not to touch.

The smoky air forced Petra to blink. When she opened her eyes again, not even a second later, the neon sign glowed faintly on the alcove's wall once more. It cast the alcove, and the man lounging in the far corner, into shades of candied violet.

The faintest rim of golden light from the rest of the bar kissed tousled curls, broad shoulders, and spread legs. It gilded his horns, too, just enough to see their wicked shape in the dark. They arched back, slightly to the side of his brow and curled, almost completely, until the sharp tips brushed his hair.

One hand held a whiskey glass to his lips. The other lifted, two fingers curling, to beckon her into the dark.

"Are you sure?" Rasmus had asked her again when she'd arrived at the bar. The man didn't owe her anything, but he tried to look out for her in his own gruff way. *"You know how dangerous that demon is, right?"*

Yes, she knew. Even though she'd been more or less out of the criminal world since it made her an orphan, she knew people.

And every one of those people feared Shade.

Petra forced her fingers to relax, to let go of the wine glass. They cramped. The rest of her did, too, as she consciously tried to ease the tension in her shoulders, her thighs, even in her face.

You're dealing with bigger predators than him, she thought, flattening her palms on the tabletop. *Buck up, buttercup.*

She stood up and shimmied, as gracefully as she could, out of the booth. Each step felt heavier than the last, but she worked hard to keep her expression neutral, her gait even, as she rounded an empty table. Her gaze remained locked on the demon, who casually sipped from his glass. There was barely enough light to see his face, but she got the sense that he was smiling.

Everything in her, every lesson she'd learned on the streets and animal instinct, balked as she crossed into that alcove.

But Petra didn't stop. She kept walking, measured and steady, around the abandoned pool table, toward him.

He'd commandeered the only table in the alcove — a small, square thing barely big enough for a couple of drinks. It was framed by two chairs on either side, turned to face the pool table but angled just enough so one could have a conversation with the person in the opposite seat.

Petra eyed the set-up, assessing possible escape routes and the distance between the chairs. Perhaps he'd chosen the chairs for the same reason she'd requested a booth from Rasmus: when dealing with a predator, it was always best practice to keep one's back to a wall.

Unfortunately, *she'd* chosen the booth because it was private but also easily viewable by the rest of the bar. *His* choice was tucked completely out of sight. If no one wandered by — and she doubted they would — then they might as well have been in their own private room.

Cold sweat dewed on the back of her neck, beneath her fall of glamoured hair. *Shit.*

The demon dwarfed both the seat and the table. Even his glass looked small in his clawed hand. He wasn't even in his shadow form and she was certain he could kill her with one strike. She got the peculiar sense that she was seeing an illusion, and that the *real* demon was bigger, more monstrous than the man before her. All that wild energy was compressed, a spring ready to release at any moment and reveal the true face of the monster.

That was a good thing, she reassured herself as she sat in the empty chair. Petra needed someone deadly. The gods knew her enemies were.

The demon rested his drink on his thigh. The large ice cube in the center clinked against the glass as he assessed her with those amber-on-black eyes.

This close, she could just make out the general shape of his features. They were even, symmetrical. High cheekbones and proud brow. His skin was pale in the faint light of the neon sign and his smile...

His smile was a thing of nightmares.

It unspooled slowly, like the drawing of a blade across a whetstone. She swore she could hear it, that distinctive *shwick* of metal on stone — a promise of pain in a sound, a *look*.

The tip of his tongue danced along the edge of sharp incisors. He said nothing, but something in the way the dark fringe of his lashes lowered over those horrible eyes made her hackles rise.

Normal people felt the impulse to fill the quiet. They hated the sound of their own thoughts. When faced with someone like Shade, they probably felt compelled to say *something*, anything at all, to fill the silence and assure themselves that he was actually like them. If they said something, he'd reply. That meant they didn't need to be so scared, right? It was the impulse of the sheep assuring itself that the disguised wolf couldn't be a wolf, no matter how odd its wool looked.

But Petra knew the game. She didn't say a word.

After a full minute had passed, the demon's smile widened into a grin. The sight of it was made all the more unsettling by the fact that she noticed he had a beauty mark above his lip. She wasn't sure why it bothered her, only that it did.

Looking at her in a way that could only be interpreted as taking her measure, he said, "You left your drink."

Her muscles coiled again. Shade's voice was not the cold, flat thing she expected. It was a deep, unabashed southern *drawl*.

"I'll get another," she lied.

Her stomach dropped at the sight of his widening grin. She'd always thought that the phrase *the cat that got the cream* was an exaggeration for run of the mill smugness, but looking at *that* smile...

The demon set the glass on the table between them. "How about we share?"

Petra didn't spare the drink a glance. "No, thank you."

He settled back in his seat, broad shoulders rounding in a careless slouch as his legs spread. They were long enough that the one closest to her nearly brushed her knee. Petra didn't give in to the impulse to move away, but she wanted to.

"Why not?"

"I don't drink hard liquor."

"Why?"

Because it's dangerous to get drunk around a predator. Because I can't afford to walk back into the temple even a little buzzed. Because if my parents hadn't ended up shot, they would have died in a bar, bottles in hand.

"Because I don't like the taste."

The demon said nothing. He pinched the tip of his tongue between his teeth and watched her, his big body as still as a corpse.

At length, he asked, "And what's your name, pretty thing?"

"Didn't Rasmus tell you?"

"Rasmus tells me a lot of things. I'd be stupid to believe even a fraction of them."

That, she had to admit, was wise. Rasmus Adams was a good man — deep, *deep* down — but he was only trustworthy if you squinted. Or if you planned on giving him something he wanted. In her case, she was desperate enough to do a bit of squinting as well as giving him what he wanted.

Or rather, *who* he wanted.

"My name's Zenna," she told him, shoulders relaxed and tone *just* the right amount of nervous.

Shade picked up the drink again. Speaking against the rim, he murmured, "And what do you need from me, pretty Zenna?"

"I need information on someone. The kind you could only get if you... say, hypothetically, broke into their suite and hacked their computers." She sucked in a deep breath as discreetly as she could. "Could you do that?"

He swallowed a sip and set the glass back down, closer to her side of the table than before. "Is that all? I'm a little insulted. You called for a racehorse when it sounds like an ass would suffice."

"An ass wouldn't qualify for this race, I promise," she replied.

"And why's that?"

"Because the man I need information on is..." Petra paused, trying to think of a way to describe him that encompassed just how dangerous he could be. "...influential. Incredibly influential. And paranoid. If I could pay someone like Rasmus to do it, I would, but I don't think they'd take the job — or live to collect."

Shade tipped his head against the grimy wall. His throat was a beautiful arch. A perfect ridgeline of muscle and bone stretching out from the black collar of his dress shirt. His lips pursed. "Mm, sounds very dramatic. Did you take acting classes when you were a kid? Bet you made a real cute Dorothy or some shit."

Petra breathed through her nose twice, fighting the urge to show him her teeth. "It's the truth."

"Now, why should I believe that?"

"What?"

In slow, languid movements, the demon rose from his seat to tower over her. For the first time since she spotted him, she noticed that he wore a black on black suit, neatly tailored and minimalist. It seemed at odds with the mop of curls on his head and yet also perfectly *him*.

When he stepped away from his chair, Petra's middle tightened, preparing her to stand up as well, to stop him from leaving until he heard her offer. Her desperation was almost tangible, oozing out of her pores like stale sweat.

Before she could launch herself out of her chair, he stepped up to her knees and casually pushed them to one side with the back of his hand.

Petra watched, bewildered, as he hiked up his slacks and dropped into a crouch before her. At last they were at eye level — and far, far too close.

The air between them wavered, just for a moment, as her magic crackled to life in response to the threat. Petra clutched the tacky armrests of the chair. *Rein it in!*

Being a luminist, a witch with the ability to manipulate light, was all well and good until one lost their temper. Then things tended to catch fire. Normally she kept fantastic control on her magic and tried to lean on that rigid self-discipline as she grappled with her emotions.

She failed, though. She could tell by the way his eyebrows rose and that smile made another appearance.

Reaching across her body to snag the glass from the table, he sighed, "Now... I'll be the first to say there's nothing wrong with lyin'. I love to lie. I try to do it every day." He swirled his drink with one hand while the other found a home on the armrest just behind hers, overlapping their limbs until he'd made a cage out of his body.

"But the thing is, Zenna, when it comes to clients, I don't like liars. There's only ever room for one of those in any relationship, I reckon, and since I'm the more skilled party here..." He tipped the glass toward her. "Why don't you drink hard liquor?"

He's fucking with me, she realized. The thought scalded her. He *had* been fucking with her, probably from the very first word out of his mouth.

If her spine got any stiffer, she worried the entire column would shatter. Speaking through her teeth, all pretense stripped away, she answered, "Lots of reasons. Most pertinent being that I can't risk it."

He took a deliberate sip. His eyes never left hers as he collected a drop from the rim with the tip of his tongue. "Does this look spiked to you?"

"Why would you spike a potential client's drink?" Petra tried to rein in her tartness, but it was hard when she needed this so desperately and he was just... *provoking* her. There wasn't any damn time for games. "I'm not worried about you drugging me. I can't afford to have my senses dulled."

"I don't have any plans to hurt you." Those glowing eyes went heavy-lidded. "Yet."

Petra's temper got the better of her at last. Leaning closer, until they were almost nose to nose, she whispered, "Believe it or not, demon, you *aren't* the boogeyman I'm afraid of."

She didn't expect him to move away, but she also didn't anticipate he'd tilt his head to one side and suck in a deep, noisy breath. As he did it, movement drew her eye over his shoulder — to the writhing shadows that blanketed the pool table and floor all around him.

"Now *that*," he murmured on his exhale, "is the truth. Stupid of you, but honest."

Petra eased back. It meant he won, but she didn't care. She wasn't scared of Shade, not really, but she also didn't have any particular desire to die by shadow strangulation that night, either. "What? Did you *smell* it on me?"

"No, I just like the way you smell." Before she could dwell too deeply on that, he asked, "What's your name?"

Her mouth went dry. It was useless to lie again, seeing as he somehow knew she'd given him a fake one, but that didn't mean she had to give him an answer. "I'd rather keep that to myself. You don't need it to take the job."

"Need it? 'Course not." Shade's attention drifted over her face, down her throat, to examine her jacket and plain blue shirt underneath. "I don't *need* anything. I don't need this job. I don't need this whiskey. I don't need your name. I don't need to see your real face." His gaze traveled back up to fix her with a look so flat, so bland, it managed to unsettle her more than that violent smile. "But I want it."

"And I want a man of reasonable skill and a healthy disregard for danger to help me before someone puts a bolt in the back of my head," she shot back.

Shade had the gall to *roll his eyes.*

Petra dearly wanted to smash the whiskey glass against one of his horns, but managed to restrain herself. Speaking tightly, she asked, "Do you want the job or not?"

He shrugged. "Y'can't afford me."

"You don't know that."

It was a smirk that played around the corners of his mouth then. "I do."

"How?" she demanded. "You can't just look at a person and know—"

A claw hooked in the fabric of her shirt, just beneath the collar. Before she could think to fight him, he'd tugged until her ear was level with his lips and she could feel the stale air of the bar against the sweaty skin between her breasts. Her gold necklace, the one she'd been too stupid to take off, dangled between them. She could smell his breath, the tang of whiskey and something uniquely him. He didn't wear cologne. His scent was subtle, raw. Oddly compelling.

His lips didn't quite touch the shell of her ear, but she could feel them moving against flyaway strands of her hair when he whispered, "Not even San Francisco's High Priestess makes enough to afford me."

A wave of nausea nearly made her sway in her seat. *How does he know?* She'd fucked up somewhere, somehow. "I don't know what you're talking about. I have an inheritance. A very, very large inheritance. I haven't touched a dime. I swear I can pay you whatever you charge me." Backed into a corner, she couldn't help but let a bit of her real desperation into her voice when she added, "You can have all of it."

He didn't move. For a long time, his only reply was another deep breath and slow exhale.

"You're scared."

"Yes."

There was no use in denying it. She'd been scared since the day she received the ashes in the mail: a neat little box with a plastic lining and a flimsy plastic plague glued on the lid.

Maximilian Dooraker, High Priest of Glory's Temple. Death in dutiful service. - 1856-2044

She wasn't sure what tipped her off, but something in his demeanor changed. Shade eased back, but he didn't give her space. Instead, he gripped her jaw with one large, clawed hand and turned her head to better peer into her face.

She jolted at the contact, her skin burning with a sudden defensive flush. The air shimmered again, more violently this time, as her magic screamed outward from the core of her being to press against the surface of skin — begging for release.

"There she is," he whispered, apparently untroubled by the way the air between them had heated to an almost unbearable degree. She could see him a little better, lit as he was by her own burgeoning glow. Too bad it made him *more* intimidating, not less.

Shade rubbed his thumb against her jaw as if he wanted to test the texture of her skin, or perhaps in fascination with the way it cast its own weak light. "The goddess's own flesh," he said, lips curled in that mocking smile. "Isn't that what they say in those press releases? *The rising star of Glory's Temple.* San Francisco's personal sunshine. And yet here she is, practically in the lap of a *demon.* How very scandalous of you, High Priestess. You shouldn't be here. Don't you know what kind of monsters play in the dark?"

Petra's breath sawed in and out of her chest. Despair crashed into anger and then mortification. The urge to cry humiliated her almost as much as his mockery.

She didn't care what Shade or anyone else thought of her. She didn't even care about whatever bullshit fluff the Temple's overzealous PR department put out about her.

All she came for, all she had existed for since the day she received those ashes in the mail was the truth. And she was wasting what little time she had left to get them on a man who had never intended to help her in the first place.

Cautiousness burned away. She slapped his wrist with the back of her hand, dislodging his grip on her jaw. "Let me go."

"No."

Petra kept her hands away from the wooden chair, afraid she might accidentally ignite it, but she felt no such compunction in regards to Shade's suit.

He let her grab his lapel, playful interest glittering in his lambent eyes. It smoldered under her palm. When thin tendrils of smoke began to mix with the clouds of cigarette smoke in the air, she bit out, "Let me *go.*"

"Are you going to burn me alive, little goddess?"

"Yes. If I have to." Petra tugged him close to whisper in a clipped, flat voice, "It's not like I haven't done it before."

It had been a long time, but she knew how to defend herself. Pushed to it, Petra could be a monster all on her own.

She was quickly learning that Shade didn't disguise his thoughts behind a mask. His expressions were mercurial, the variations of his smile endless. When he looked at her then, it was with a grin that was positively *wolfish.* "It won't look very good to your adoring worshippers to see their favorite priestess running away from the scene of a crime, would it?"

"They wouldn't know it was me."

"They wouldn't?" He lifted his glass to his lips again and took a long sip. "You're awfully recognizable."

"No, I'm not—" The words died on her tongue.

There, hanging on either side of their faces, was her curtain of blonde hair.

Petra released him with a hard shove, but he didn't do more than a slight rocking back on his haunches. His laughter grated against her pride like broken glass.

She hadn't even felt the glamour's release. Too late she recalled the way he'd rubbed her skin — no doubt wiping away the carefully concealed, skin-tone sigilwork she'd painted there to anchor the spell.

Petra stood quickly enough to send her chair back into the wall with a dull *thunk*.

A burning desire to say something, anything, to wipe that smug look off of his pretty face ate away at her gut, but she'd already wasted too much time and effort on him.

Casting the demon a scathing look, she made to step around him, toward the small door that led to the staff area.

Except she couldn't move.

Shadows coiled around her legs, holding fast, as Shade took a leisurely stroll around her. He leaned against the pool table, drink in hand, and gave her another knife-like grin.

"Tell me your name."

Already caught and too angry to care, Petra blazed bright in the artificial darkness he'd summoned. *"Fuck you."*

He clicked his tongue. "Stubborn. I like that. Can cause some trouble, though. I like that, too."

She wanted to hit him. She wanted to hit him and hit him and hit him until she couldn't lift her arm anymore. "If you were never going to take the job, then why are you even here? Why are you doing this?"

"I never said I wasn't gonna to take the job," he replied, "only that you can't afford my fee. Even if you think you can, I don't want your money."

All at once, the wildfire inside her went up in smoke. "What do you want?"

"Tell me why you're so scared and maybe I'll share."

The urge to hit him came back with a vengeance. Speaking

through her teeth, she explained the situation a bit like she was speaking to an unruly five year old. "The man I need information on is powerful within the Gloriae."

He almost looked disappointed. "So you're worried about losing your cushy job."

That almost startled a laugh out of her. *Worried about my job?* Gods, she never even wanted it in the first place. The only reason she joined the Temple was because of Max and the only reason she became San Francisco's High Priestess was to discover what happened to him.

Despite what everyone around her thought, Petra Zaskodna wasn't ambitious. She was a survivor so exhausted by treading water she'd resigned herself to drowning. A rat who'd chosen to get on a sinking ship.

All at once, the fight bled out of her. Petra closed her eyes, her glow dimming until it vanished completely, like a candle snuffed by the darkness that held her. "Can you do it or not?"

He frowned, eyes narrowing. "'Course I can." The bastard didn't even give her time to feel relief before he added, "But I want something more valuable than money in return."

Dread trickled, drop by drop, into her veins. "What?"

The demon swirled his drink, mostly melted ice now. All the while, she could feel his shadows creeping up her legs, the ghost of a touch, until they'd wrapped around her waist. She forced herself to keep still, not to panic at the feeling of delicate constriction. "I've heard rumors that you have connections to a certain Sovereign's Consort."

She didn't need to think about it. "Absolutely not."

"You don't even know what I want from her," he protested without heat, as if he *knew* she'd react vehemently and thought it was awfully funny.

"I don't care what it is, you aren't getting to Margot or the sovereign through me."

She might've been a liar. She might have conned her way into being San Francisco's High Priestess. She might have forged a relationship with Margot Goode on a pretense, to dig for information on the Elvish Protectorate's involvement in Max's death.

But she was damn loyal to the people who earned it.

Margot considered her a friend. They were both new to the city, and though they were witches with vastly different backgrounds, there was a connection between them that had blossomed into a friendship. Constrained by her quest and the lies it forced her to tell, Petra hadn't been able to give that relationship the amount of herself it deserved, but that didn't mean she would throw Margot under the bus.

Shade rolled his eyes again. "I don't want her liver. I just want access to the m-generator." He paused. "Or its blueprints. Either one."

Petra only vaguely understood what he was talking about. A week or so prior, the media had been set aflame by the news that there'd been a breakthrough in the field of m-energy — the study of magic and its use as a clean energy source.

People had been trying to figure out a way to capture magic from the atmosphere for at least a thousand years, so it was big news when an unknown witch announced that she and her research partner — another Goode, *surprise, surprise* — had solved the problem with a state of the art generator.

There'd been some hub-bub about the EVP volunteering to completely fund the first prototype right there in San Francisco, as it was a city that had historically suffered due to the destructive nature of atmospheric magic. At that point, Petra had stopped paying attention.

Even so, she knew enough to understand that there was no way on Burden's green Earth she would be able to get Shade anywhere *near* that prototype.

"I can't do that," she sighed, more exhausted with every second that passed. "I really can't. Even if I would *ever* put Margot in the same room as you, it still wouldn't work. That generator will be the single most intensely guarded thing on the entire continent."

Although Margot might be a close second. She shuddered to imagine what the sovereign would do if he found out she'd allowed a man like Shade anywhere near her. She had a teeny-tiny soft spot for elves, but that didn't mean she was stupid. The sovereign could pop her head off her shoulders as easily as a kid's fist crushes a to-go yogurt.

Shade made a sucking sound with his teeth. "Ah, it was worth a try. Good thing I want something else, then."

Pushing back on the pool table, he stood up straight and closed the distance between them. Shadows crawled up his legs, too, but they didn't stop at his waist. Instead, the tendrils slithered up his arms and around his chest to consume his whole body up to the neck. There they stayed, moving restlessly along the base of his throat, as if they had a mind of their own.

"Tell me your name." This time there was no playful note in his drawl.

"Why? You know it."

He blinked slowly, once, but his expression didn't change. He was very still. "I want you to give it to me."

She could only stare at him. This meant something. The entire conversation had been an assessment of her, and now she felt like she was being tested on a subject she didn't even know if she'd studied.

"Petra," she rasped, at a loss. "My name is Petra."

And there was that slow, violent smile again. Her heart beat faster at the sight of it. She couldn't tell if her body wanted her to run away from it or, for reasons she couldn't possibly comprehend, run *toward* it.

The shadows curled around her right hand. She watched, disconcerted, as they lifted it up just in time to accept his nearly empty drink.

Using two fingers, Shade guided the glass to her mouth. It rested there, cool and wet from his lips, when he murmured, "There's a good girl. Now drink."

For the life of her, Petra couldn't understand why she did it, but she did.

There was hardly any alcohol left. It was the aftertaste of whiskey that touched her tongue, carried by a sip of cool water. Whiskey and something like... him.

Shade's gaze lingered on her for a moment, the look in his eyes completely inscrutable, before he stuffed his hands in his pockets and stepped around her. Had she passed the test or failed?

She had no idea, but something told her he'd *won.*

The shadows followed him, drawn like the ends of a cloak toward his body and away from her in a slow, steady drag. Something deep and neglected in her stirred at the sensation even as her arm, bereft of his support, fell limp by her side. The cool glass dangled from numb fingers.

"You're leaving?" she croaked.

"Sure am." He passed her. On his way, he pulled one hand out of his pocket to flick her hair off her shoulder.

Petra whirled around. "But you didn't say what you wanted?"

He gave her a pitying look, like he thought she was a little slow on the uptake. "Didn't I?"

"No, you didn't."

"Hm." He kept walking. Shadows pulled away from the walls, the table, the floor. Like miles of black gossamer, they folded and draped and slithered back to him.

Petra watched with wide eyes. She'd met demons before, but never one who could manipulate shadows like *that.*

"Wait," she gasped, lunging for his arm. "Are you going to help me or not?"

Shade patted her hand once before he pried her fingers off of him, one by one. "I'll help you, but right now I'm leavin'."

"How can I get a hold of you?"

"You don't."

She was very, very close to stomping her snakeskin boot. Or crying. Either one. Maybe both. "How is this supposed to *work?*"

Shade cast her a boyish smile over his shoulder. "You don't get a hold of me and you don't do the work. That's my job. Don't worry, little goddess, I'll find you."

Petra could only watch, helpless and confused, as those long legs took him out of the bar. Behind her, the lamp flickered back to life.

Read Devotion's Covenant!

ALSO BY ABIGAIL KELLY

Find all new releases, bonus chapters, and exclusive content on the Works by Abigail Patreon! If you just want to keep up with what's going on, then sign up for Abigail's newsletter.

FRAGILE BEINGS: A NEW PROTECTORATE NOVELLA COLLECTION

In the first volume of The New Protectorate Stories...

Fate can't be contained.

#376: A fey Changeling is rescued from captivity by a reluctant demon

on a quest to find his fate. Of course Dom expects trouble, but he is shocked to discover his fate is tied to an imprisoned fey woman. Charlotte's a kicking, spitting, hissing little Changeling — and she's his.

A dragon's kiss burns cold.

Astray: When Paloma Contreras, arrant scientist, accidentally dooms a rogue dragon to death, she'll do anything to save his life. If that means giving up the mountaintop she's called home her entire life, so be it. Too bad Artem Aždaja has no plans to steal her roost. He only wants one thing: *her.*

Desire fogs the mind.

Weathering: Elise Sasini, an intrepid reporter and weather witch, sets out to uncover the story of San Francisco's legendary sentient fog and gets a lot more than she bargained for. The mysterious elemental agrees to tell his story in exchange for a taste of the life — and the woman — he craves.

Three novellas. Three couples. One fractured world. Step into a magical near-future where love builds, breaks, and defies boundaries.

Available in Kindle Unlimited, ebook, and paperback!

Empire: The New Protectorate Stories: Volume Two

Love blooms in the dark.

After a lifetime of service to the Amauri vampire family, retired assassin Harlan Bounds lives his life exactly as it pleases him – on his private estate, surrounded by beauty, and unbothered by the bloody politics of the criminal underworld he left behind. He doesn't need or want for anything... except, perhaps, the tantalizing witch hired to look after the acclaimed rose garden on his grounds.

Zia North has nursed a crush on the mysterious vampire that is her boss for nearly a year. They've never spoken, and she knows the rules by heart: never stay on Empire Estate's grounds after sundown and never, *ever* bother Mr. Bounds. There's no chance for her to fulfill her sensual fantasies, so what's the harm in indulging a crush that will never see the light of day – or the kiss of darkness?

It's all daydreams until she makes a mistake that finally brings her face to face with the intimidating vampire. Harlan's dark intensity draws her in, and Zia's light sparks a craving that can't be denied. Fantasy clashes with reality when his dangerous past threatens to bite them both, but not even the violent conflicts of the vampire syndicate can sever a bond forged in blood.

Available in Kindle Unlimited, ebook, and paperback!

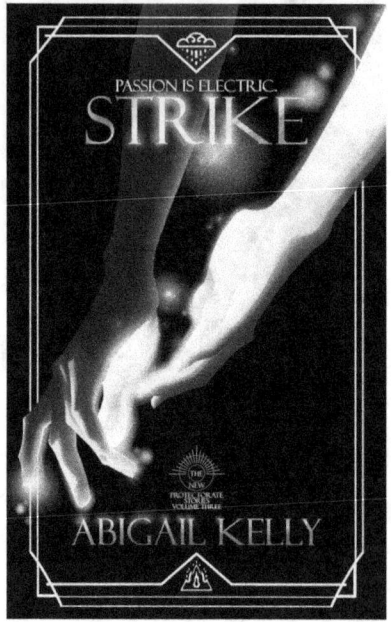

STRIKE: THE NEW PROTECTORATE STORIES: VOLUME THREE

Passion is electric.

After a millennia of longing, Hele has finally gotten her chance to live. A lightning elemental with a voracious hunger for knowledge and experience, she takes to her new life with a gusto that surprises everyone she meets. After two years of learning how to navigate the world she's been thrust into, Hele is only missing one thing: love. She wants one particular dragon, but when he turns her away, she decides that life is too short to wait.

Vael has been a loyal soldier of the Draakonriik for a century. He's never wanted anything more than to serve his clan and his leader... until the day he snatches a beguiling elemental from the sky. For two torturous years, he's resisted the call of his Chosen, trying to give her a chance to fly before he claims her and hides her away in his nest.

But when Hele decides to set out on a quest to find a mate, that resolution goes up in smoke. His lovely elemental is about to learn a very valuable lesson: a dragon will do *anything* to win his Chosen.

Available in Kindle Unlimited, ebook, and paperback!

VITAL: THE NEW PROTECTORATE STORIES: VOLUME FOUR

There's power in connection.

Josephine Wyeth has only ever known the shadow of war. Sheltered by her father's secretive work, she exists as both prisoner and caretaker as the violence creeps ever-closer. Once powerless, now she is something else: a new being crafted by her father's cruel hands, proof of his genius and threat to all who meet her. She's desperate to escape, but with no friends and the horrors of war lurching toward them all, her future is bleak.

There's no hope — until the day she's thrown in a cell with her father's latest experiment.

Otto Beornson, a fierce shifter from the wilds of the Northern Territories, is the latest in a long line of victims captured from the front and shipped to her father's laboratory. He shouldn't be any different, but when they meet, their fates intertwine in a way no one could have expected. Standing on the brink of an abyss, their blazing connection is a lifeline.

He'll do anything to save her, even if that means giving up his soul. She'll do anything to free him, even if it means becoming the monster her father always hoped she'd be.

Available in Kindle Unlimited, ebook, and paperback!

GLOSSARY

A full character directory and map can be found at Abigailkkelly.com

PLACES

United Territories and Allies: What we would consider the continental USA. A loose federation of sovereign states established after the Great War. The UTA capital is United Washington, in the Neutral Zone.

The Elvish Protectorate: Also known as the EVP. Stretches from Oregon to New Mexico. Capital city is San Francisco. Led by the elvish sovereign Theodore Thaddeus Solbourne.

The Coven Collective: Also known as the Collective. Encompasses Washington state. Capital city is Seattle. Led by a large coalition of witch covens, with Sophie Goode acting as their leader.

The Orclind: Encompasses much of the Midwest. Led by the Iron Chain, a close-knit government made up of orcish clans and family groups. Capital city is Boulder.

Shifter Alliance: Takes up a section of the midwest and all of the south. (Unfortunately includes Florida.) Run by a very, very loose alliance of shifter packs from three capital cities — Minneapolis, Oklahoma City, and Atlanta.

The Draakonriik: Also known as the 'Riik. The second smallest territory, it takes up all of the Great Lakes region and stretches to New York. Led by Taevas Aždaja, the *Isand* (ee-zand) of the dragon clans. Pronounced: *dra-kon-reek*

The Neutral Zone: Also known as the New Zone. Technically it is held by a coalition government consisting of representatives from the UTA, but in reality it is run by a syndicate of feuding vampire families. It is a small strip of land squeezed between the Draakonriik and the Shifter Alliance.

GODS

Light & Darkness: The primordial gods who created all the others. Also known as The Lovers and First Union. Both are generally represented as female.

Loft: God of the sky and creator of flying beings. Twin sibling to Tempest. They know no gender. Also known as the Boundless One.

Tempest: God of the ocean and creator of all water beings. Also known as the Hungry God and the god of love.

Burden: God of the Earth, creator of all beings who live within it — most notably the orcs. Husband of Glory.

Glory: Goddess of sunlight, magic, and creator of elves. Worshipped by witches for giving the gift of magic to humanity.

Blight: God of forested places and disease. He works in partnership with his daughter Grim and shares her dominion over demons and all reviled creatures.

Grim: Goddess of death. Known as the Merciful One and the Brilliant Lady. She is widely beloved.

Craft: God of change, newness, and messengers. Creator of humanity and viewed warily by non-worshippers as the Chaos Maker. They change their gender frequently, but generally is referred to using he/him pronouns.

TERMS

Alpha: a broad term used by many communities generally associated with a leader — either of a small family group, a pack, or even a territory.

Anchor: a vampire's mate. Anchors are carefully chosen and usually longterm-to-permanent arrangements, as they take considerable energy to make/become. A vampire must inject their venom into a host many times before their blood chemistry adjusts such that they become unsuitable for consumption by another vampire and their sleep cycle switches to a nocturnal pattern. At this point, they can can also produce/carry to term a vampiric child. Temporary anchors do exist, although they are relatively rare due to the intense withdrawal symptoms associated with ending the regular venom intake.

Arrant: someone born without m-paths, or the ability to channel and use magic.

Burnout: the colloquial name for the degenerative medical condition caused by excessive magic in humans. Over time magic can damage nerves and brain tissue, which will inevitably result in death if not treated with with development of a witchbond.

Change: an elvish term for a sudden shift into adulthood. This is marked by 5-14 days of "madness", usually triggered by some stressful event around the age of 16-18. The elvish body is flushed with hormones to the point where sudden growth, overwhelming hunger, and aggression take over. Viewed as an incredibly vulnerable time, only immediate kin are charged with the care of their loved ones — which includes isolating them, preventing harm to themselves/others, and feeding them. The change marks the second phase of an elf's life, when they are no longer coddled children but young adults who can accept challenges and family responsibilities. Formal adulthood is attained at 30.

Changeling: a term first used to refer to fey children fostered out to non-fey homes, now more widely used to mean any person raised by people who are not the same beings. *Ex:* A dragon couple raising a human child.

Chosen: the formal term for a dragon's mate. The act of finding a mate is called *Choosing,* and is considered sacred.

Consort: an elvish mate. A term used exclusively by elves to refer to someone they are biologically compelled to pair up with. This usually involves intense sexual attraction, but can vary from person to person.

Dragon: a person with a dual form. In their bipedal form, they have claw-tipped wings, horns, and a tail. In their quadrupedal form, they are roughly the size of a standard SUV and can fly at extremely high altitudes for weeks at a time. They come in a variety of extremely saturated colors that shift with the time of day (light to dark). They breathe cold blue fire and can see the

Earth's magnetic field. Identifying mating feature is marked change in behavior, including the overwhelming urge to nest.

Elemental: a being created by a spontaneous magical eruption. They often take on the attributes of whatever weather they happen to be born into, *i.e.* a lightning storm might produce a lightning elemental, or a blizzard might make a snow elemental.

Empath: a person with the ability to feel and manipulate the emotions of others.

Elf: someone born with jewel-toned skin, claws, pointed ears, and four fangs. Very secretive and considered apex predators who require a strict hierarchy to function. Average height of 6-7ft. Identifying mating feature is the retraction of claws.

Fever: shifter mating imperative triggered by the "animal's" choosing of a mate. Marked by a perpetual near-shift — elevated body temperature, increased aggression, build-up of magic, and the compulsion to mark. A shifter displays their readiness to find a mate by creating a den.

Fey: a person with nearly vestigial, insect-like wings, small fangs, and claws. Usually live in large groups. Identifying mating feature is bioluminescence.

Foresight: the ability to see multiple possible futures. The average number is between 2-4, with the likelihood mental instability increasing with each subsequent possible future.

Great War: a conflict between the territories of the North American continent that began in 1817 and ended in 1917 with the signing of the Peace Charter, which established the United Territories and Allies of modern times.

Halfling: the elvish term for an elf with mixed heritage.

Healer: a person who possesses the ability to see into and heal bodies through touch.

Isand: the title of the leader of the Draakonriik. Pronounced *ee-zah-nd*

M- : M- is frequently used as shorthand to denote when something is infused or otherwise combined with a magical element.

Marriage Sigil: a custom symbol branded into the foreheads of spouses (pairs or multiples). Each one is unique and infused with a small amount of magic as a reminder of the power love holds. They are typically sought out by worshippers of Glory — mainly witches and arrants. Elves, though worshippers, don't usually take a marriage sigil when they find their consorts or form a unions with other elves.

Mate: a catchall term for a significant other. Used by many cultures, it has varying degrees of weight. To shifters, orcs, and demons, the word mate is synonymous with family, monogamy, and dependence. It is much more loosely used within arrant society, as well as amongst elves, who generally prefer the term *consort.*

Met: acronym for *magically enhanced tech.* A branded home assistant that can do everything your Alexa can, as well as small, low-level magic to help around the house.

Metallurgic Inoculation: a vaccine given to all elves within hours of birth to make them immune to iron poisoning.

M-siphon: a containment device used to imprison a magical being and siphon off their magic. Highly illegal.

R-siphon: also known as *reverse siphon.* New technology that redistributes magic away from the siphon instead of into it.

M-lev: a play on *maglev,* meaning a high speed train that levitates using magnets. In this case, magnets *and* magic.

M-weather: magic weather. Very common, but can result in "clusters" or storms that wreak havoc if not properly contained. In rare circumstances, it can also produce a sapient being known as an *elemental.*

Orc: a person with green, gray, russet, or blue skin, two fangs, and claws. Widely renowned for their strength and beautiful voices. Identifying mating feature is "the kohl", or altered, dark pigmentation of the hands and feet developed after meeting their mate.

Pixie: a small, winged creature with compound eyes with about the same level of intelligence as a rat. In the wild they live in trees and in burrows, but have adapted to living in walls, pipes, mailboxes, etc.

Pull: elvish mating imperative. A sudden hormonal shift caused by exposure to a compatible partner's pheromones, marked by the retraction of claws and volatile mood shifts. The pull is only "satisfied" when hormone binding occurs — the term for long term exposure to a mate, resulting in permanent biological dependence on their pheromones. This process increases fertility and often results in the conception of multiples. Lack of exposure to a mate can cause severe physical reactions (lack of appetite, muscle pain, headaches, insomnia) as well as the deterioration of mental stability.

Shifter: a person who can shift into an animal form. They can partially shift (changing only parts of their bodies at will) and often take on characteristics of their other half. Famous for their strength and tenacity, as well as their dual-voiced "shifter purr" which many people find deeply attractive. Usually found in packs.

Sigil: a symbol used to channel magic. Western countries use the alchemical alphabet formally codified in the 1800's, though many, many variations are used all over the world.

Sovereign: the title of the ruler of the Elvish Protectorate. It is capitalized when used in place of a name.

Turbo Virgin (c): Theodore Thaddeus Solbourne, Sovereign of the Elvish Protectorate and Head of the Solbourne Family.

Union: an elvish marriage. Usually done for financial, political, or procreational benefit. The parties involved are not fated or biologically compelled to be with one another, and might have many lovers or even a consort outside of their union.

Vampire: a person who drinks blood to survive and cannot go out in sunlight. Vampirism can only be "caught" with the exchange of fresh blood, and as of 2045 is much more widely spread through procreation. Vampires can only breed with their *anchors.* Identifying mating feature is marked change in behavior, including overwhelming desire and need for total isolation.

Ward: a magical barrier with varying levels of protection. A ward can be something as simple as a proximity alert — "someone walked into my garden" — or as complex as full on defense — "someone crossed the threshold and has now burst into flames". The severity of the ward depends on the complexity of the sigils used to create them, and wards can have many layers, each one with a unique purpose. Personal wards can also be used, such as in clothing or embedded into jewelry, though they tend to be expensive and difficult to foolproof.

Were: a person infected with the were virus, a much mutated strain of the vampirism virus, resulting in altered physiology and magical ability. They can be identified by their heterochromia, or different colored eyes. They are the newest magical race and viewed warily by the general public for a variety of earned and unearned reasons. Identifying mating feature is marked change in behavior, including highly increased territorial instinct and the urge to nest. Pronounced *ware.*

Witch: Humans with the ability to use magic, which is passed down genetically. A person needs to be born with m-paths (a unique nervous system) to use it, however, humans were not initially adapted to use magic safely. Geneticists believe they acquired the ability through interbreeding with other beings. This interbreeding resulted in many unique qualities, such as the massive variety of abilities, power levels, and unique skills known to select families. However, it is also responsible for "burnout", which is the degenerative neurological condition a witch with mid-to-high level power will experience if they do not share their magical load with another being via witchbond. Witches are classified from least to most powerful — brightling, brilliant, and gloriana.

Witchbond: a magical bond formed between a witch and another being. Due to the nature of magic and humanity's much more recent adaptation to it, witches of *brilliant* and *gloriana* power must form a bond with another being usually beginning around 150-200 years old. This bond filters magic through the other being, neutralizing its damaging effects and reducing the chances of burnout to almost none. This bond also gives a power boost to the partner. A witchbond is permanent and can only be severed if one of the partners dies, at which point the surviving partner can form a new bond. Though commonly associated with a romantic partner, a witchbond is not inherently romantic and can be shared with a friend, sibling, or (ill-advised) an enemy.

PRONUNCIATION GUIDE FOR NAMES OF IMPORTANT CHARACTERS IN THIS BOOK

Carmine Safi: kar-mine sa-fee

Atticus Caldwell: at-ih-kus cawld-well

ABOUT THE AUTHOR

 Abigail Kelly is a writer and illustrator of alternate histories, love stories, and women with drive. Her work is heavily influenced by both her modest family roots and her passion for history. Her favorite authors are Shirley Jackson, V. E. Schwab, Ursula K. Le Guin, Kresley Cole, Nalini Singh, and just about anyone who writes about the weird and wonderful. She lives in San Francisco with her dog, Babs, who remains stubbornly illiterate.

Content Warnings

Content warnings: in-universe purity culture, in-universe religion, withholding of food as punishment, virginity, human trafficking, death of parents (past), adoption, handling of dead bodies, blood, organized crime, violence, murder, breeding, and explicit sexual content.

www.ingramcontent.com/pod-product-compliance
Lightning Source LLC
Chambersburg PA
CBHW060641260626
47161CB00008B/2949